MW00961648

When Wishes Were Horses

When Wishes Were Horses

Cynthia Voigt

GREENWILLOW BOOKS

An Imprint of HarperCollinsPublishers

When Wishes Were Horses

Copyright © 2024 by Cynthia Voigt

All rights reserved. No part of this book may be used or reproduced in any manner whatsoever without written permission except in the case of brief quotations embodied in critical articles and reviews. Printed in the United States of America. For information address HarperCollins Children's Books, a division of HarperCollins Publishers, 195 Broadway, New York, NY 10007.

harpercollinschildrens.com

The text of this book is set in 11-point Sabon.

Book design by Paul Zakris

Interior illustrations by Ramona Kaulitzki

Library of Congress Cataloging-in-Publication Data

Names: Voigt, Cynthia, author.
Title: When wishes were horses / Cynthia Voigt.
Description: First edition. |
New York : Greenwillow Books, an Imprint of HarperCollins Publishers, 2024. |
Audience: Ages 8-12. |
Audience: Grades 4-6. | Summary: Four kids who live in the same town but do not know one another are mysteriously connected by magic when they are each granted two wishes.
Identifiers: LCCN 2024004846 (print) | LCCN 2024004847 (ebook) |
ISBN 9780062996923 (hardcover) | ISBN 9780062996947 (ebook)
Subjects: CYAC: Wishes—Fiction. | Magic—Fiction. | Family life—Fiction. |
Friendship—Fiction.
Classification: LCC PZ7.V874 Whe 2024 (print) |
LCC PZ7.V874 (ebook) | DDC [Fic]—dc23
LC record available at https://lccn.loc.gov/2024004846
LC ebook record available at https://lccn.loc.gov/2024004847
24 25 26 27 28 LBC 5 4 3 2 1
First Edition

GREENWILLOW BOOKS

For all of us,
every one

CONTENTS

How do such things happen? Something appears, sudden as disaster. It wasn't there and now it is.

An envelope arrives, in your mailbox, on your dinner table, your dresser, your computer keyboard. It's in your hand. You are alone when it finds you. No one else sees it, to ask about it or take it from you. There is only your name on the envelope.

Inside, two pieces of pale gray tissue paper, each the size of a playing card, and simple instructions:

ONE WISH AT A TIME
WHISPER IT TO ME
BE WISE

Magic?
Impossible.
But what if . . . ?

BUG

ONE

A few years ago—not long before you were born—a boy called Bug was living in the apartment over the family sports equipment store on Garden Street, a couple of blocks down from the park. Bug's parents had opened the store only a year earlier so there was a lot to get done every day, what with jobs, and schools, and the work of keeping house for a family of eight. They all had busy lives but they ate suppers together almost every evening.

One Sunday in October, when they had filled their plates with roast chicken, mashed potatoes, peas, and gravy, Sissie asked Nana if she believed in magic.

"Good question," Nana answered, the exact same thing she had said when Bug asked her if Santa Claus was real, back when *he* was the littlest.

It had rained all day and Sissie, who only liked cartoons, had watched their old DVD of *Aladdin* twice through. "If I had three wishes, I'd wish for a magic carpet," she told them. "And I'd take us all to Disney World. Plus the Grand Canyon. Then to the beach, the ocean beach, because nobody's ever seen the ocean."

"Not true, sweetheart," Dad said. He called his youngest child sweetheart whenever she pulled his heartstrings by being even more adorable than usual. Bug had only ever been Bug, a name given to him by his sister Mary. When Mary first saw him, when he just got home from being born, she had said, "He looks like a bug!" and burst into tears.

"You don't mean that," Dad said but Mary did, because Bug was a scrawny thing with long skinny arms and legs and big round eyes.

"Maybe you could take him back and get a fat one instead?" Emma suggested. She was too little to know better.

"A bug!" Mary wailed, because she understood about babies, how they couldn't be taken back to where they came from.

"It happens that I've seen two oceans, the Atlantic and the Pacific," Dad told Sissie, "and your Nana once spent a whole summer on Cape Cod, working as a waitress, didn't you, Nana?"

What would I wish for? Bug wondered.

"A whole summer when I was fifteen," Nana said.

"That's where I found that big scallop shell you children used to play with in the bath, at my house." Because she was old, and a widow, and loved them, Nana had sold her house, giving some of the money to Dad to help open the store. She planned to live with them until she could buy a retirement house with her sister.

A Porsche or a motorcycle, Bug decided. But it would be years, six to be exact, before he could drive.

"I remember!" Sissie cried. "The shell was as big as both my hands!" Everybody smiled at her, Bug, too. She didn't know anything much but that didn't bother her. Also, she was short and round and happy, with curly hair and a high voice and it cheered you up just looking at her. "The carpet could take us to mountains, after. What's the highest one we can go to?" Sissie asked.

"That would be Mount Everest," Bug told her. He liked being someone who knew things. Maybe he should wish to be the smartest kid in his class.

"And we'll stand on the very top, holding hands, and we'll be able to look down and see the whole world," Sissie promised them.

"There's a problem with that," Adam told her. "Because when you go up really high, the clouds are below, blocking your view." Adam was the oldest of them, already a junior in high school.

"Also, it's really cold on top of Everest, or any high mountain," Emma added.

"And there's almost no oxygen to breathe," Mary added. "It's dangerous."

"Not if it's a wish," Sissie assured them. "Not if it's magic and we're holding hands."

Or maybe Bug would wish for a swimming pool. Except that would need a backyard so maybe it should be a house with a swimming pool and he could invite his friends over to swim.

"That's the thing about magic, Sissie," Nana said, a little sadly, as if this was bad news for her, too, even if she was so old she had to know better. Bug knew better about magic (there wasn't any) and it turned out he knew better than Nana, because the next thing his grandmother said was, "Magic can backfire on you. It can trick you."

"But that's not fair," Sissie protested. "Mom?" she asked, as if her mother could fix the unfairness of it.

"It's only dreaming, magic wishes, and what's wrong with dreaming?" Mom asked.

"But if it *was* real? What would you wish for? Do you ever think of that?" Nana wondered. She turned to Dad to ask him in particular. "Hank?"

"That's easy; I'd wish for a van," he answered. If

he had a van with the store's name, street address, web address, and phone number on it, it would be not only a free advertisement wherever he drove, but also a way to solicit new business from—for example—golf courses who had to have golf balls for sale, and also sports clubs who needed jerseys and equipment, and country clubs which had golf courses *and* tennis courts *and* swimming pools. Also every school had a sports program and every sports program needed equipment, which a sports store van could deliver right to their doors. "I know we've been open just over a year so business isn't good enough, but when it is I'll get a van and quit the school-bus-driving job."

"I thought you liked driving the bus," Adam said. "The kids think you're cool."

"I like it well enough," Dad agreed. "The kids are fun, and it's a good job for now because the hours match up with slow times in the store so Mom can handle things on her own there. I'm not complaining, I'm just wishing. Just pretending magic can happen. What would *you* wish for, Adam?"

"A forty-eight-inch smart TV," Bug said, although nobody was asking him.

"I'd wish to be accepted into AP Calculus," Adam said.

"I thought you'd already signed up to take it next year," Mom said.

"I did, but signing up isn't getting in. I'll never make an A in trig and Mr. J doesn't let anybody into calculus without an A in trig."

"Then you should wish for an A in trig," Mary pointed out.

"I'd wish for a really fancy Lego set," Bug said. "The kind with more than a thousand pieces."

"There's no room for something like that in this apartment," Mary told him.

"I'd build a castle, a medieval castle, with everything they really had in them," Bug said.

"He could use my bedroom floor," Nana offered. They had given her the biggest bedroom because she was the oldest.

Mom was stuck on Adam's wish. "You always get As in math," Mom reminded Adam.

"Trig is really hard, Mom, and calculus is important. You have to have it for any real science, or engineering, too."

"Or an iPhone," Bug said. "I'd wish for an iPhone so I could play games on it."

"Even if you had one, you need to pay every month for data," Mary told him. "You have to buy games.

It takes money, and you can't get a job until you're fourteen," she reminded him. "Although you could baby-sit."

"No thank you," Bug told her. Baby-sitting was definitely not cool. He could wish for an iPhone already loaded with games, couldn't he?

"We don't have to ask Mary what she'd wish for," said Emma. Mary might be a ninth grader, practically grown up, but she had wanted the same thing since her first pony ride, when she was Sissie's age.

They all knew what she'd say but Mary said it anyway. "A horse." She knew she'd never get one. Not only was a horse expensive to buy, but if you didn't have your own farm—if you lived in an apartment above a store, for example—you had to pay to stable it. She saved up her allowance and any baby-sitting money she earned, which was enough for about one riding lesson a month, and she was greedy for more. But what are wishes good for if you can't be greedy?

"And we all know what Nana's wish would be," Adam said.

"What else?" Nana laughed. She knew that her real wishes were impossible: that her husband was still alive, or that everyone in the world would stop polluting the planet, and hating one another for no good reason, and instead start helping one another out of difficulties. "I never planned to live with you for so long. Don't get me wrong, I love it, really I do, it's just—"

"We love having you, Nana," Dad interrupted, and at the same time Mom said, "You're a real help, Mom, especially this year with opening the store. Plus, we enjoy your company."

"Still," Nana said, "if Sally's house had sold, you two could have the big bedroom and I'd have moved with her into one of those warmer-climate residential communities so you could come for vacations. Free holidays in the sun, think of it. That would make it a win-win-win wish."

Mom agreed. "The good news is that sooner or later, Aunt Sally's house will sell and that particular wish will come true. No magic required. Whereas what I'd wish for is truly impossible." She put on a mysterious smile and waited for their questions, teasing them.

They waited back, teasing her back. It was Bug who gave in. "What? What would you wish?"

Mom laughed. "I'd wish I had a talent."

"A talent?" Mary wondered. "Do you want to be an artist?"

"You're a genius at being my wife," Dad said.

"Do you want to be someone famous?" Emma asked. "But who'd be our mother if you were famous?"

"Don't worry, it's not happening," Mom answered, untroubled.

"Cowboy boots!" Bug cried. He'd just thought of that and he remembered the boots John Wayne wore in a movie he'd watched with Nana. He'd really liked those boots, and if he had a wish he could have a pair and walk around in them the strong, calm way John Wayne did, and be the hero of the story.

"Cowboy boots are cool," Adam agreed.

"You'd be taller, too," Emma added. "Girls like boys to be taller," she explained, because she was in middle school now and had started thinking about boyfriends.

"Who said anything about girls?" Bug demanded.

"Your time will come," Dad promised him.

"I've got better things to think about," Bug told them. "Like—a skateboard! That's what I'm wishing for."

Adam punched Bug lightly on the arm. "You've already saved almost enough, remember?"

"If I wished for a skateboard I could get a better one and use what I've saved for a pair of cowboy boots.

Leather ones, and fancy. How much would that cost?"

"You always have something more to want." Adam laughed. "He does, doesn't he?"

Nobody denied it, but Dad said, "Don't knock it. It's liable to make him rich."

"If he gets rich, we can all go live with him in his fancy house," Sissie announced.

"I'd wish for curly hair," Emma told them. Nobody was surprised to hear that. "No, for a cat."

"Why not a dog?" Mary wondered. "I'd like us to have a dog."

"That can be *your* wish, then," Emma said.

A pet wasn't a bad idea. "I'm wishing for a scary, cool pet, like a wildcat, so when I take it to the park . . ." But Bug couldn't really imagine a wildcat at the end of a leash, and when everybody else said, "I wouldn't do that, if I were you, Bug," he had to agree with them. "Okay, but it has to be a big dog," he said. Really, he didn't know what he'd wish for.

Would you?

TWO

Bug had almost no alone time in his life. Their five-room apartment had no quiet corners, no private nooks, no locked doors. If you like a bustling, busy, noisy family life where if you feel sad there is always somebody to notice and offer to hug you or play War with you, you would like that crowded apartment. Luckily for Bug and his family, they all did.

People crowded around Bug outside of home, too. Bug walked with his brother and sisters to catch the bus to school, because the high and middle and elementary buses all had the same pickup location, the corner of Garden Street and the park. At school there were kids, of course, plus teachers and administrators, plus any stray adult who happened to be in his vicinity, a parent, crossing guard, janitor, or lunch lady, a customer in the store. He had lots of friends and when the weather was fine enough to hang out in the park, he could always rope in enough people for a scrimmage, even if Peter and Mark refused to play in a game that had girls. Even if he'd never seen them before, Bug didn't mind asking someone if they wanted to join in. "Doesn't matter how good you are," he promised and they believed him, maybe because Bug had such matchstick arms and legs, or maybe because there was something in his face that told them this wouldn't be the kind of game where people yelled at you or quarreled over calls.

With all these people crowded into every waking moment of his days, you can see how hard it was for the wish envelope to find Bug. Eventually, however, in the middle of one dark night, Bug woke up. *Something,* he thought, staring up at the darkness that hung over his bed on the top bunk. *What was it?* Not a bad dream, he decided, because bad dreams leave streaks of scaredness. He hadn't dreamed about a fanged, winged, clawed monster, or a tsunami, or trying to hide from a school shooter. His heart wasn't beating fast; his legs didn't feel like they wanted to run.

Neither was it the kind of good dream where you start falling but then spread your arms and fly, floating in air as if it was a swimming pool. It felt to Bug almost as if he'd laughed himself awake, except he hadn't.

In any case, he'd need a glass of milk to get back to sleep so he went down the ladder. He didn't worry about waking his brother in the bottom bunk. Adam was hard enough to get out of bed in the mornings after a full night's sleep. He'd never wake up just because the door opened.

But as soon as he took one step into the kitchen, Bug entirely forgot the dream and his glass of milk because an envelope lay on the kitchen table with his name on it. His actual name, in capital letters, STANLEY WHITSTABLE. Bug almost didn't understand that it was for him because of that, which was pretty funny, so he was grinning as he lifted the flap—it wasn't sealed; lucky it still got delivered—but now that he thought of it, had he seen his address on the envelope? He didn't waste time checking. He pulled out the folded piece of notepaper and opened it and two thin, gray, playing-card–sized pieces of tissue paper slid onto the tabletop.

It took only a single glance to figure it out. He had two wishes, and he'd make them by whispering into the tissue paper. Bug knew what his first wish was. "I wish I had . . . " He hesitated, doing the math, not wanting to look greedy. "Two more wishes." That would give him the same number of wishes plus one extra to always wish for more wishes with. That was pretty clever, if Bug said so himself.

Except nothing happened—if you didn't count the tissue paper getting sort of pinkish and warm in his fingers.

Except the tissue really had changed in both color and temperature, so it had to be real magic and Bug was smart enough to guess it didn't much like what he'd asked for.

Okay, that made a certain amount of sense. Bug thought for a minute and then raised the tissue to his mouth again to whisper, "I wish I had a million dollars."

This time it turned red and got so hot that he dropped it onto the table, licking his fingertips and then blowing on them.

Except they didn't look burned, and they weren't.

The two tissues were still waiting right in front of him, so everything was okay. Bug decided he must have missed some special instructions, telling you the kind of wishes you weren't supposed to make. He also thought that probably he'd better make his next wish stick to the rules, whatever they were. There had been something more written that he hadn't actually read, he remembered, and he reached for the notepaper. . . .

It was gone.

So was the envelope.

He knew he hadn't thrown them into the recycling

bin, but he looked anyway. He also looked under the table, then under the refrigerator, the stove, and the dishwasher. The envelope and the note had both just disappeared.

This was both good and bad; bad because he didn't know what the rules were about, and good because it proved this was real magic. Raising the tissue to his mouth for the third time, Bug whispered, "I wish I had a skateboard."

The tissue disappeared. Bug smiled, pulled his wallet from the backpack that was packed and ready by the door, and slipped the second wish paper into it, between the two dollars he had left from his allowance. That all taken care of, he went to bed. He didn't need a glass of milk to get back to sleep.

It wasn't even a day later that his father got a notification from *Skater's World* magazine announcing a giveaway program for all the independent sports stores in the region. The magazine and the manufacturer were going to donate three Apex top-of-the-line skateboards, as well as knee and elbow pad sets and helmets, for each store to give away by a lottery. You didn't have to buy the lottery tickets; you just went to the store, filled in your name and phone number on a printed ticket, and dropped it through a slot into the big black box they provided.

"Why would they do that?" Bug wondered (but you know what he was hoping). "Apex is the best brand; they don't need to give their boards away."

"To increase sales," Adam suggested, and Mom added, "Raise interest in skateboarding."

"It's good promotion for all three of us," Dad added, "store, magazine, and manufacturer."

"It's also free advertising," Nana pointed out.

"Does it really say free tickets?" Mary asked.

"It's a genuine giveaway," Dad told her. "UPS will be delivering the gear tomorrow afternoon."

"You could give me one of the boards and still have a drawing for the other two," Bug suggested.

"That's cheating," Nana scolded.

Dad agreed with her, and so, actually, did Bug, which is why he didn't argue when Dad said, "You'll put your name in the box like everybody else. If you do win one, I want it to be fair and square."

It already wasn't fair and square, Bug knew. But he wasn't about to tell anybody that. And two Saturdays later when his father drew his ticket out of the black box that held the names of about every kid in the elementary and middle schools, as well as a number of high school skaters and even a couple of adults, Bug kept on keeping quiet. The magic had made his ticket the second one selected. Bug pretended to be surprised. He didn't have to pretend to be excited, or glad, and he took the board right to the park. There, he spent the rest of the Saturday, and all of Sunday, practicing. He rode on the flat paved paths first, until he could balance easily (there was some falling off before that happened because the Apex was livelier than any other skateboard he'd borrowed). Then he tried skating along the paths with inclines, and he managed just fine going down, although he couldn't figure out how to go uphill. He'd have to get Brad and Kenneth to show him how. Bug practiced Sunday afternoon, too, and Monday morning he rode his new skateboard to school. It felt really good. Before this, he'd never been one of the lucky ones.

THREE

Kids were watching as he entered the schoolyard, dismounted smoothly, and then smiled around at everyone, like a rock star or an astronaut. That they didn't smile back, not really, Bug didn't notice, any more than he noticed the way Mrs. Hannigan didn't congratulate him. She just waved him in the direction of the closet where skateboards were stored during the school day so they wouldn't get stolen or ridden in the halls. But he *did* notice the way Tony and Brad and Kenneth kept silent. He noticed and decided they were just jealous. He knew they'd put their names into the box. He knew also that Brad had put his in more than once.

("Ten times, so I've got a ten times better chance than you three twerps," Brad had boasted. When Kenneth said that was cheating, Brad shrugged and told them, "Everyone cheats, if they can get away with it. Haven't you noticed?" "How'd *you* get away with it?" they wondered, so Brad explained how he'd put his first ticket in when Bug's mom was at the counter, again when it was his dad, and once Adam, then how he sent his two little sisters in with one ticket apiece, his own dad once, and two grown-up cousins for eight. "I got your sister Emma to take one in for me and there was this old lady going in to buy soccer shoes for her granddaughter for her birthday. And that's ten," Brad had concluded. "Ten's my lucky number.")

See? Cheaters don't win, Bug wanted to say to Brad. He wanted to say that and give high fives to Tony and Kenneth. But they all gave him *looks* as he set down his tray and sat in the last empty chair, so he didn't say that, or anything else, because when your friends act unfriendly you can't not notice it. Bug noticed it and noticed it until finally he gave up on ignoring it and demanded, "Spit it out, you guys. You're jealous I was lucky."

"Lucky?" Brad asked. "Lucky? You're saying you were just lucky, and not a close relation of the man who owns the store and drew the winning tickets?"

"Yeah. I am saying that. And I didn't enter any ten times, either, like somebody I could name."

But nobody at the table even made a murmur of agreement with this.

"You don't actually think we . . . ?" Bug demanded.

"Think it was fixed?" Tony said. "*Everybody's* wondering. You can't blame people for being suspicious."

"My dad would never—never ever—cheat," Bug announced, and he knew that was true. But he wondered if using magic meant that *he'd* cheated, in a way. He knew he hadn't. Any cheating had been done by the magic. He was innocent, he knew. But was he really? If he had had magic on his side? "There's not much I can do about it now," he told his friends. "Anyway, can we meet up at the park after school? And you could show me how to do a kickturn?"

Nobody answered him. They were all intent on their lunches, two plates of chicken fingers and fries and one thick ham-and-cheese sandwich in a baggie, three chocolate milks, three bananas. For the first time in ever, Bug was glad they only got twenty minutes for lunch, because he could hear what their silence said. It wasn't as if they'd stop being his friends; he knew that. It was just the Apex skateboard they didn't like, not him. They'd get used to it, he figured.

Except they didn't. They still hung out together at school but his friends must have gone to some other part of the park to skateboard, because they didn't come and join him in the usual places. Neither did they ask him to join them somewhere else, or talk about someday practicing on real ramps and jumps. The lucky Apex was turning out unlucky.

Even at home, his mother remarked at the end of the week that the store hadn't enjoyed the increase in business they'd expected from all the publicity around the lottery, the newspaper coverage of the drawing, all the talk beforehand and all the people coming to the store to drop their names in the box. When she said that, she looked at his father and raised her eyebrows. Dad shrugged and everybody was suddenly concentrating on their own plates. But didn't they know as well as Bug that no cheating had been involved?

Even though he expected that Tony and Brad and Kenneth would avoid him, Bug went ahead to the park on Saturday morning. But he didn't do more than ride, sometimes along the paths, sometimes on the sidewalks that ran all the way around it. On Sunday he stayed home to watch *Aladdin* with Sissie and play a long game of War with Emma. He thought maybe he'd ask his parents what he could do to fix things, but he knew they'd tell him to just ignore it. He asked Nana instead, because he had to ask someone, because it really bothered him, because he hadn't done anything wrong.

"That's hard," Nana said, but she didn't offer any advice.

Monday morning, satisfied to flip the board smoothly up into his hand at the curb and walk to the next sidewalk, Bug skated to school and ignored the sideways glances from other kids and the way his friends pretended the subject of skateboarding didn't exist. He'd decided what he'd do. He'd tell his parents that night and in the morning he'd post the announcement at school. People who wanted the Apex could put their names into a bowl on her desk and at the end of the week Mrs. Hannigan would be the one to draw out a winner's name. That way, things could go back to normal, and maybe business would even improve. That decision made Bug feel better. It was like he'd been pulling a heavy sled through deep snow up a steep hill and now he was at the top. He felt like he didn't want to have this skateboard even though he knew that without it he was going to have to go back to saving up for one. He planned to enjoy his last afternoon with a top-of-the-line board, and practice the kickturns he'd been studying on YouTube.

You can probably predict what happened. He powered up for a kickturn, but not enough, and the board fell away from under his feet and clattered on the concrete. Bug landed—hard—on his right shoulder and had to lie there for a minute—it was no longer than a minute that he lay there; the wind hadn't been knocked out of him—before he sat up. *More practice needed,* he told himself, embarrassed, and then he remembered he was giving his board away in the morning and he stopped caring about being embarrassed because things were about to be fixed. He glanced around for his board, but it was gone.

How far off could it fly? Bug wondered, looking and not seeing it.

One of the girl skaters, probably an eighth grader, explained it to him. "They rode away on it, they're like—a gang? You won't see it again," she told him. She didn't sound at all sympathetic. "They said if you can't even do a kickturn that board's too good for you," she added, as if she agreed with them, and when he told Kenneth and Tony and Brad about it the next day they said, "Sucks, man," but as if they thought he deserved to have the board taken away from him. And then, eventually, it all blew over, the way quarrels do between friends.

Later, when he had grown up (older people do this, and you will, too) Bug would tell his Apex skateboard story and smile, describing his ten-year-old self flat on the ground and the Apex being spun away never to be seen again. At that time, however, the only reason he didn't start crying right then and there was the way that eighth-grade girl was looking at him. He guessed what she was thinking. "Yeah, well, you're wrong about that," he told her, getting angry instead of sad, and he turned away, walking, going home without a skateboard.

"My board got stolen," was all he answered when they asked him why he came in late. "I'm okay, these things happen, I'm fine," he told them, when he could see they were going to start getting worried at him. "It doesn't matter," he assured his family.

Having learned his lesson with the skateboard, Bug took his wallet from his backpack, closed the bathroom door behind him, and wished for the Lego set. When, a week later, Nana presented him with not only two ten-pound bags of assorted Lego pieces (that made *eight thousand* pieces!) but also a special bin to keep them in, nobody seemed to feel this was unfair. "My bedroom floor is yours," she told him and all he could say was "Thank you, Nana," because he really really was grateful, even if it was actually the magic at work.

If it *was* the magic. If you believe in magic.

For once, Bug did something slowly. He enjoyed all the different steps, reading up on everything medieval castles had in them and drawing the plan, locating the pieces that would fit together not just to make walls and a tower but also a chapel and a central well as well as stables for if there was a siege. He drew up a plan, concentrating hard, sketching out ideas, humming to himself, before he fit the first two Legos together to begin the tower. He worked on his castle almost every day, for weeks, once he'd finished the day's homework, his fingers busy and concentrating so hard that a couple of hours could be gone before he even noticed. He worked hard, but it wasn't hard work; it was restful, a lot more relaxing than watching TV. Bug sat on Nana's floor, building his castle and humming and sometimes even—if it was a tricky part—talking to himself. "Don't rush it, you'll ruin it if you rush."

By Christmas, he'd completed it and his family was impressed by his castle and his persistence.

For all of the time this took, Bug was pretty content. The model meant that for weeks he had something to look forward to and something to do that he wanted to do. It also meant that he spent a lot of time with Nana, who would read or knit or just talk with him while he worked. In fact, Bug was there when Sally called with the good news, so he was the first to know that her house had been sold, which he guessed because Nana kept saying, "Congratulations," and "Yes, South

Carolina, the climate looks mild, don't you think?" She also said, only once during this conversation Bug wasn't actually eavesdropping on because she knew he was right there, listening, that "They'll be glad to have me out of their hair." Then she said her goodbyes and congratulations again and hung up.

"No we won't," Bug disagreed, without thinking, and Nana said, "I know and I'm going to miss all of you, that's for sure." Then she explained something about Sally's children living in California but Bug had just had an idea about how the drawbridge could be improved so he didn't listen to what his grandmother was saying, the way you don't listen to your grandparents when they ramble on. He was enjoying this second wish more than he had been able to enjoy his first one.

FOUR

If you think it happened because Bug was cruising around on his new skateboard (not an Apex, but the best he could afford with the money he'd saved) you'd be wrong. You'd be closer to the truth if you decided that the weeks he spent taking apart his medieval castle to offer the pieces to a shelter for homeless families made him think of it. Mixed in with those two was the gladness of a spring Saturday, when bursts of daffodils appeared in the new grass at the park, and Bug, having mastered the kickturn, was working on ollying while he waited for Kenneth and Tony and Brad to show up. Somehow, that morning in the park, Bug got thinking. Really thinking, about what had happened. What he'd done wrong.

Because when he really thought about it, it was clear that he'd been unimaginably lucky: he'd been given two wishes that were real magic. He'd had them in his hand. And he had wasted them. Not only did he not have an Apex, but also (not that he regretted it) he'd given away the Legos. He could have made things different, but he hadn't.

The store did a steady business but not enough for his father to quit driving the school bus; Aunt Sally hadn't yet moved, so Nana was still living with them; Adam had *not* been invited into the calculus class; Mary was no closer to having a horse than a monthly riding lesson could bring her; and Emma hadn't been able to get her parents to agree to any pet bigger than a goldfish, which definitely didn't count as a real pet. Mom didn't start painting pictures, although a couple of times Dad called her "Genius Lady" to get her laughing, and it goes without saying that Sissie hadn't found herself being carried off on a magic carpet. Nothing had changed and that was all Bug's fault. He could have wished for any one of those things other people had wanted and he hadn't, had he. Instead, he'd wished himself a skateboard that came with so many bad feelings that he was glad when it got stolen, and then for a toy that lasted no longer than winter. In fact, the thing he'd enjoyed most from his two magic wishes was passing the big box of Legos on so someone else could enjoy it, too.

Bug had been given two magic wishes and he'd

ended up with nothing and he finally figured that out on a spring morning in the park. If Kenneth hadn't appeared right at that moment, pumping his board up to top speed, Bug might have turned into an unhappy ashamed and regretful little puddle right there on the sidewalk. He wished he'd used his wishes better.

Because what else can you do if you'd been given two real magic wishes and all you'd done was waste them?

FIVE

For the rest of that day, while he was riding with his friends and helping out in the store until closing, then having supper with his family and watching TV, Bug forgot the sad thing he'd finally figured out. He fell asleep as soon as he got up into bed.

But something woke him up. Something just felt . . . wrong? Not exactly right?

Bug climbed down the ladder and went into the kitchen for a glass of milk.

No envelope addressed to him waited on the table. No wishes. Not that he'd expected any. Not that he deserved any.

From half a block away, the streetlamp barely lit the kitchen and that suited the uneasy, regretful way Bug was feeling. He poured himself a glass of milk but didn't drink it. Knowing that he had wasted his two wishes was a dark, heavy feeling, even worse than when everyone was convinced he'd cheated for the

Apex. He moved to the window and looked gloomily out into the gloomy night.

When the kitchen light turned on, Bug snapped around. But he saw right away that it was only his brother so he said, "That's my milk."

"I'm having crackers and peanut butter," Adam answered.

Adam sounded as gloomy as Bug was feeling. "What's with *you*?" Bug demanded.

Adam shrugged. "Nothing."

Bug guessed he knew the something that was the nothing Adam was talking about. "Did they tell you what you should have done to get into AP Calculus?" he wondered.

"I didn't ask."

"Why not?"

"I'm not a complainer."

"Is it complaining to ask why?"

Adam shrugged again. "Or a whiner."

"Why is it whining to understand what you need to learn to be good enough?" Bug asked, a little cross with his brother. "Besides, don't you need calculus for college courses?"

"I'm not so sure I'm going to end up going to college. I can't see why I should. If I'm not a good enough student even for a high school AP course I'll never make an engineer, or scientist. So college would be a waste of money."

Bug knew something about how bad it felt to waste things. "I guess," he agreed.

"Although," Adam said, and hesitated. Then, "You could be right. I mean, if there's something I need to know and I don't even know what it is, I haven't got a chance. So you're right, I *should* ask. I mean, what can it hurt? He's already turned me down. Thanks, Bug. I guess I really needed to see this from a different angle. Because I don't want to give up on the whole rest of my life because I didn't make an AP class and never even asked why."

Adam left the room without even turning out the lights, so Bug did that and in the comforting dimness drank his milk, still feeling bad, although not quite as bad as before.

Adam didn't waste any time talking to Mr. J. "He asked me a lot of questions and a lot of them I had to say I didn't understand, didn't know the answers to," Adam reported at the dinner table. "I can see now why I didn't make it."

"I'm proud of you for trying," Nana told him and Mom and Dad said the same.

Adam agreed. "Yeah. I guess I'm proud of me, too. Even if it didn't do any good."

But if Adam wasted no time asking, Mr. J wasted no time answering. The next day, Adam came home with good news: he was going to be taking AP Calculus in his senior year, after all. Mr. J had actually complimented him. "He said that someone who knows what he doesn't know and asks for help to learn? He said that makes me his kind of mathematician." Adam grinned and accepted their congratulations.

This definitely made Bug feel a lot better. It wasn't the same as not wasting his own wishes, but that ship had sailed. Bug had to accept it and so he did. Accepting it, making himself accept it even if he didn't want to, also helped him not feel nothing but bad.

Besides, he couldn't help seeing that he wasn't the only person feeling bad. More and more often, Mom wasn't her usual cheerful self. This really bothered Bug because Mom was his mother and he needed her to be happy. He wanted her to like being in charge of the apartment and to enjoy helping out in the store and to feel lucky she was the mother in his family. What did she want when she wanted a talent? One afternoon, he came into the kitchen where she was chopping and slicing vegetables for a stir-fry, humming to herself as her fingers lined up carrots to slice them into matchsticks. It was the humming that made Bug start asking questions.

"Mom?"

"Umm," she answered, her attention on her hands.

"Do you like cooking?"

"What kind of a question is that?"

"No, because you're really good at it even though you have to do it all the time, for all of us, and you never get bored and everything always tastes good. So I was wondering because isn't cooking a talent?"

That got her attention. "What?"

"You're really good at it," Bug insisted, "and it's not easy, is it?"

"You're just used to what I make," Mom answered. "Or you want something. What is it now, Bug?" she teased. "A BMX bike? A bigger TV? Since you're here, why don't you set the table."

But at dinner she announced, "For Christmas this year I want a pasta maker, one with an electric engine. Because there are so many of us."

"*Mom*," Emma protested. "It's not even summer, it's months until Christmas."

"They're pricey, aren't they?" Dad asked.

"That's why I'm telling you now. You might want to all club in on it," Mom said. "I can try making cannoli too, not just pasta."

Everybody began to think of what Mom could make that they'd like until Dad said, "Why do we have to wait until Christmas to eat all this? Nana, are you in?"

"She's always been a good cook," Nana agreed. "She's worth it."

"Really?" Mom asked. "Do you mean it?" and her eyes lit up.

"Really," Dad and Nana said together.

"I can help!" Sissie announced. "What's pasta?"

That was when things changed for Bug. He felt as if a paintbrush had washed the entire world over with brighter colors. It started with Mom's lit-up eyes and it just kept going, until it became the kind of person he was, someone who tried to figure out what people would wish for and waited patiently for an idea of how he might help them get it. As the years passed, the person he had changed into made a good friend and a good boyfriend, a good employee, a good son, a good brother. . . . Not perfect, he never aimed for perfect, or even for best.

Good was good enough for Bug, and for the people lucky enough to know him.

Would you have guessed that of the three wishes Bug made, the most valuable one would be the one that had no chance of being magic?

ZOE

ONE

"Admit it: you think I should be doing everything."

That was her mother.

"I was only saying that I have a job too."

That was her father.

"You actually expect me to be the primary bread-winner and do the shopping and laundry, housework, carpooling, doctors, dentists. . . . You expect me to do everything."

"You know that's not true."

"I suppose you resent my not cooking."

"Oh no, I don't miss that."

Her mother was a terrible cook.

And they were off.

Not that they were ever not off, these days. They'd kept going off for . . . a long time. *How long?* Zoe wondered, as things went along the way they always did these days, when her parents were in the same room. Her mother attacked and her father gave ground until he reached the point where he wouldn't back off any longer. The dinner table was the worst, she thought, seeing Connor put his fork down on his plate. In about two seconds he'd ask to be excused to go to the bathroom, and not come back.

Zoe kept eating. Dad was a good cook, and she liked chicken parmesan. Besides, she had no trouble chewing and swallowing while her parents fought away over her head.

Once they were off, they couldn't be returned to . . . What was the opposite? Not on, unless it was like game on, but wasn't that the same as setting off? Like racehorses? Actually, she was tired of the way her parents weren't getting along. Why couldn't they get over it, instead? They didn't used to fight so much; she was pretty sure of that. Also, they didn't used to fight like this.

". . . the kids, we shouldn't . . . ," her father said.

"I hate your trick of hiding behind the kids, Evan," her mother snapped.

Because if they'd just stop fighting, everything would be okay again.

"I gotta go can I be excused."

That was her brother.

"I'm not hiding, Ali, I just think that killer instincts

belong in court, squeezing all you can get out of failed businesses. Not here in our kitchen."

They fought ugly now, her parents. It used to be they needled and squabbled, mostly; sometimes they seemed to get along just fine; then there'd be something—an election, a request for the class parent, an in-law—and they'd be having an ugly fight. Other kids' parents fought, or so the kids said. Whether they fought like hers or not, Zoe couldn't say; she'd never seen any other kids' parents fighting and now she couldn't ask a friend because she'd stopped having good enough friends to ask over before fourth grade.

Zoe twirled spaghetti on her fork, forked the bite into her mouth, and ignored them. Connor couldn't, but he was only in second grade so maybe he was too young? Besides, Connor's head was . . . worse than in the clouds. It was in the Milky Way, with his planet mobile and his posters of their entire solar system, of the night sky in their hemisphere, and one with every fact anybody knew about Venus, where Connor thought there could be life. No atmosphere fit for humans had been discovered there, but who knew what was waiting behind the thick layer of clouds that shielded Venus from even the strongest telescopes.

Connor talked like he was already some space scientist, some Mr. Spock or astronaut.

Zoe figured she was an earth-onaut. In six and a half years, when she was old enough to vote, her and everybody else her age, she knew what she'd be voting for: clean air, clean power, clean water, and better schools. Not that hers was bad but she had heard of some seriously terrible ones, schools that didn't even teach people to read, with teachers who didn't want students to think and especially to disagree with them, who actually disliked kids. She'd vote for endangered species, too, and stopping climate change or at least slowing it down: Zoe would be voting for those.

But that was six and a half years away and she had right now to get through.

"I have to get—" Mom said as she pushed her chair back from the table. "Or I'll—" and she was gone, out the back door while Dad was still saying, "I know you do, go ahead, Ali, it's okay."

They heard the sound of the garage door going up, then a car, driving off. Zoe and her father looked at one another without speaking. They both knew this was Mom's way of letting her fury ooze out, rather than having it explode all over the house. Zoe did the same thing, only on her Rollerblades. Because of traffic she wasn't allowed to cross streets, but she'd ride around and around the block, until the flashing energy of her emotions got a little used up; sometimes it took eight or ten full circles to do that, but it worked. Dad drew back, like Connor. But unlike Connor Dad would only retreat so far. When he got that far, he stood firm. Connor, on the other hand, might not be even halfway through a plate of spaghetti (one of his favorite meals), still, he wouldn't stay in the same room with a quarrel. "They could wait," he pointed out. "It's not as if they don't have their own room."

"You don't understand," Zoe told her brother.

"I know," Connor agreed.

Then Zoe felt as if she was the one who didn't understand. "No you don't," she snapped.

Connor shrugged. He knew what he knew. Zoe puffed out an angry breath and left the room. She wasn't about to be a person who backed away. Zoe faced trouble. She fixed things—that was the kind of person she was. When something was going wrong— the TV remote, a text that disappeared from a phone, or even the time she caught Sandy copying her test answers in math—she set out to fix it. She took what- ever she knew—about how remotes work, what phone settings do, what her father had told her about why people cheat in school—and applied it, stubbornly and often successfully, too, to whatever the problem was.

Connor didn't do that. He backed away, like Dad. The trouble was, he wasn't a grown-up. He hadn't figured out the place where he could stand firm. All he had figured out was how to back away.

The trouble behind that trouble, she suspected, was these Ugly Fights.

Zoe had learned from her father that the school counselor's job was to help kids when they needed it, maybe with a particular teacher or maybe other kids, all the things kids had to deal with and sometimes even really serious things, for which the counselor had to call in child welfare or a psychologist, or in extreme cases, the police. Family problems, too, she knew. Not that her father talked about any specific kid he'd advised. He did, however, talk about kids' problems "in general," and how a counselor could be helpful. Zoe knew she could talk to Mr. K. But she also knew that in their school district, the counselors all got together twice in every marking period, to talk about their work, in case anyone had any good ideas about a different approach, or they could identify a trend moving through all the schools that was dangerous.

This meant that Mr. K knew her father. So if she talked with him about the way her parents were fighting, Mr. K would know something personal about her father that her father didn't know he knew. Which wasn't fair to Dad, was it?

Zoe didn't want to be unfair to anyone. There was already too much unfairness around, in the world, and in her own house. Angry people didn't care about being fair. So she needed a way to ask Mr. K's advice without letting him know who she was talking about.

She wished she could talk to Jayleen and Kimmy about this, but they were no longer the kind of friends they used to be. Once, they'd been a trio, with sleepovers almost every weekend and constant texting, all three of them one another's best friends. School shopping together for notebooks and pencils, working on projects together for school, together at the pool in summer, the ice rink in winter. . . . The first Christmas when Zoe couldn't call Jayleen and Kimmy to talk about what they'd gotten was the loneliest holiday she'd ever had, even though she'd been given the exact headphones she'd asked for, and a sweater with sparkling stars scattered all over it, and a hundred dollars from her grandparents. And Kimmy, as she found out once school reopened, had been given a kitten.

Zoe had never met that kitten. Muffin was her name and she was black, with three white paws and a white stripe down from one ear to her white bib. She had never met her not because there had been a big fight between the girls, or because they weren't still friends because they were, just . . . They were only school friends now, not best friends, not since Zoe's ninth birthday sleepover, the summer before fourth grade, and the way Jayleen had been frightened and Kimmy's mother arrived early in the morning, before they had even had their waffles with real maple syrup, to pick up both girls and her friends felt sorry for her, she could see it, because all during their pizza dinner, and birthday cake with chocolate ice cream, and present opening, Zoe's parents were having an Ugly Fight.

After that, Zoe stopped inviting friends over. She pretty much stopped having friends.

When you don't invite anybody over, they don't invite you back: that's a rule. When people feel sorry for you, they don't want to spend time with you: another rule. When you are embarrassed and ashamed of the way your parents fight, you don't want to tell anybody, so you're stuck with your secret, and good friends don't have secrets like that: also a rule.

Nobody at school noticed anything. Zoe was just

the same, good grades, good homework habits, good manners. Inside, she was twisted up and unhappy, one big knot, because . . . because it was all wrong, her family was all wrong, and so was she. The best she could do, the absolute and only best thing, was to face it. No whining, no complaining, and no kidding herself. She could do that, couldn't she? She was doing it every day.

Except now Connor had gone back to sucking his thumb. It was as if he'd backed so far away from the fights that he was back to being about four, and didn't want to have to get any older. As if he thought going back to not understanding anything that was going on around him would make him feel better.

Although, maybe it did? Maybe it could?

Even so, it wasn't right. If he'd backed away into his planets and galaxies, Zoe wouldn't have been bothered. Maybe. If he'd started saying he'd been to Venus, or even pretended he was a Venusian left on Earth by careless parents, she might have gone along with it, like when he had an invisible best friend living in his closet. She couldn't tell about might-have-beens, but she did know that being bothered about her brother added to how bothered she was about her parents. It made her feel sick, all the time, and wrong, too. Sick and wrong. Wrong and sick. Bad.

Was it that she didn't love her parents enough? Was she a bad daughter? Except she did love them, both of them.

Her parents, she decided, simply didn't understand how bad all their fighting was, and not just for her, for Connor, too. But how do you get your parents to understand something like that?

That was the kind of question the school counselor was there to answer and Mr. K was known to give good advice. He was her only hope.

During both lunch periods, Mr. K waited in his office, ready for company. Everybody knew this in the same way that nobody knew exactly when Mr. K had his own lunch, or what the name was that was so long he didn't want you to waste time saying it. If you asked, he'd say it for you, and laugh at the expression on your face. When Zoe knocked on the frame of his open door, Mr. K was seated in an armchair, reading. "Hey, Zoe, hi. Come on in. Do you want the door shut?"

She closed the door and took the other armchair. She'd figured out a way to ask her question without invading her father's privacy, so she started in right away.

"I've got a friend—she asked me to ask you—she's embarrassed to ask for herself and she's my friend so I said I'd do it."

He nodded and waited, all of his attention on her. He believed it, she decided, and continued. "She has this problem with her parents. They're— Her parents are doing something that really bothers her. And she doesn't know how to get them to stop."

"Hard on her," he commented.

"Yeah," she agreed. "Do you know anything she can do about it?"

"That sort of depends on what it is they're doing. Does she think she's in danger?"

"Oh no. Nothing like that."

"And you agree that she's safe?"

Zoe nodded.

"Okay, then. Good. Do you know what it is?" he wondered.

She nodded again. "Nothing illegal," she promised him. Counselors needed to be sure of that, she knew.

"So it's not illegal and she's not in danger. What about them? Will they hurt one another, the parents? Does your friend worry about that?"

"She doesn't."

"You asked her specifically?"

Zoe thought fast. "My dad told me, we were talking about his job and he said the first thing he had to establish was if anyone was in danger of being hurt. Because if anyone was, there were things the law said he had to do."

"Protocols," said Mr. K.

She nodded as if she knew the word.

"Hmm," Mr. K said, still watching her.

"I thought— We did, we talked about it, me and my friend— We wondered if a counselor might have an idea what she can do. To get them to stop. Her parents," Zoe said. "Is there any therapy trick you know?"

"Didn't you ask your father?"

"No." Zoe thought even faster. "My friend is embarrassed. I think she's sort of ashamed of the way her parents are behaving, but anyway she's shy, really shy, you know? See, she knows Dad and she doesn't want anyone to know. That's why I told her I'd ask you for her."

"Hmm," Mr. K said, with a small, friendly smile.

"Do you? Do you have an idea?" Zoe asked. She thought he must.

"I do. But it's not a sure thing. Well, with human beings, nothing is a sure thing, but . . . Parents love their children, and they want their children to think they have good parents. But parents don't always know what their children are thinking, or how they are feeling, because children don't always tell their parents things because . . . Sometimes children don't tell their parents things just *because* they love them, you know?"

Zoe did. You didn't want to worry your parents, or make them sorry to have you for their kid, and wish for a better one, someone smarter or more popular, more athletic or brave.

"Parents do the same thing, you know. So, sometimes, the children need to tell the parents how something makes them feel. So the parent can understand. Because parents can be unaware of that. For example, if you're on a team and your parent argues with the umpire, or yells at your coach, or even yells at you? Or worse, yells at one of your teammates."

"They don't, but I see what you mean," Zoe said.

"There is one really important piece of advice you can give your friend," Mr. K said. "Unless—do you know if she blames one of the parents and not the other? Or does she have a favorite?"

Zoe shook her head no, and no. She waited.

"In that case, she could try talking to both of them.

At the same time, I mean. Explaining to them both at the same time how she feels about whatever it is."

That didn't sound hard. "That's how to get them to stop?"

"It might. There's no guarantee, Zoe. Not with human beings. But I don't see how it can hurt. Often, when parents can see something from the child's point of view? That can make a difference."

Zoe stood up. "Thank you, Mr. K." This might just work. Like her dad, Mr. K had studied about people.

"Tell your friend . . . that she can always come herself to talk to me. But she doesn't have to. She has you to listen to her. Someone listening is important. Someone who believes what you are saying."

"I do believe her," Zoe could honestly say. "I really do."

TWO

It was good advice Mr. K gave her, and not just because it made her feel understood. It also gave Zoe the sense that there *was* something she could do to fix the ugly fighting. She decided to be smart about following the good advice. She'd wait for Sunday morning, she decided, the time they argued least often. They always went out on Saturday, for a date night, and the friendliness of that often lasted into the next morning. This was most true when they went out to a party. If it was only dinner, or a movie, they could wake up quarrelsome, but that Saturday they'd been invited to a dinner party to introduce the new wife of somebody Dad knew from college. Zoe easily ignored their usual quarrels ("You didn't used to take so much time trying to look younger than you are," "Am I supposed to apologize for having lived long enough to need more makeup than I did at twenty-one?"), knowing that Sunday breakfast would be a good time. Also, their regular baby-sitter, Mrs. Chester, always brought her miniature collie so she wouldn't have to "drive home alone in the dead of night." Baxter wanted to sit in your lap and be petted, wait by your chair and be fed nibbles when Mrs. Chester wasn't looking, and sleep nestled up against Connor in his bed until Mrs. Chester took him home with her.

Mom preferred other baby-sitters. "The dog sheds," she reminded them at dinner on Friday. "I trust the woman completely but I just wish she'd come without the dog."

"His name's Baxter," was Connor's response.

"Myself, I'm grateful not to have to drive someone home when all I want to do is crawl into bed," Dad said.

"You always vote against me," Mom said.

"Besides, I'm the one who vacuums," Dad pointed out.

Connor excused himself to go to the bathroom and didn't come back.

Zoe sat it out.

All Saturday evening, she anticipated talking to her parents, stopping the ugly quarrels. She felt perfectly happy, sitting beside Mrs. Chester on the sofa, Connor and Baxter at their feet, all of them immersed in *Happy Gilmore*. She definitely felt hopeful the next morning at the breakfast table, where Mom complimented Dad, "You make the best scrambled eggs," and his answer was "Special for you."

They were seated in their usual places, the parents facing one another, Zoe and Connor side by side on the bench. Connor, who didn't like eggs, didn't stay long; he drank his juice, ate three slices of toast with strawberry jam, and went up to his room, and his galaxies. When it was just the three of them, Zoe took a deep breath, and did it. "Mom?" she asked. "Dad?"

They looked at her.

"Because I don't think you understand how me and Connor—"

"Connor and I."

This was her mother.

"Connor and I," she echoed. "Understand how it makes us feel."

"You need to let Connor speak for himself."

This was Dad.

"Okay. Me. I mean I? Because it makes me really unhappy when you argue. Fight. The way you do."

Her parents looked at each other.

Zoe waited.

Mom said, "Everybody fights, Zoe. You've had fights with your friends, haven't you?"

"What do you mean unhappy?" Dad asked.

"People can't be expected to get along all the time. And—especially for a woman, a girl? It's important to be able to stand up for yourself," Mom said.

"Can you specify?" Dad asked. "Sad? Angry? Anxious?"

"We don't really fight, you know. I'm never afraid of Dad and you're never afraid of me, are you, Evan? It's never a fight-fight, not violent."

"I don't think that's what Zoe means, Ali. Or is it all of them, Zoe? Sad and anxious and angry? It's important to try and put the right name on your feelings."

"I just wish you wouldn't fight," Zoe insisted.

Mom looked at Dad. "I can't let someone just . . . steamroller over me."

He looked back at her. "Don't you ever let anyone tell you what you're feeling, Zoe."

"I really wish you wouldn't," Zoe said again, but her voice had gotten small. So much for Mr. K's helpful advice. Before she actually started to cry, she got up from the table.

"Zoe? Clear your plate!" Mom called after her.

"Can't you ever let anything go, Ali?" Dad asked.

"Somebody has to teach our children good manners," she answered.

And they were off.

They didn't say anything to Zoe, not when she turned back to get her plate, not when she rinsed it and her glass and put them into the dishwasher, not even when she mumbled, "I've got homework," and went down the hall to her room.

By then, her mother had scraped her chair back from the table and was heading for the door, and the garage, and her car.

Zoe sat at her desk and didn't even turn on her computer. She didn't take her reading book from her backpack, or her math folder. Flat hadn't been one of the choices her father gave her, but flat was how she felt, flat and boneless. Flat and floppy. And gray. If Dad asked her now how she felt, that's what she'd answer. She didn't have the energy to do anything, even play a game of sudoku. She just sat there, a flat, floppy, gray mess. Not even black, which was for terror. Or maybe it was red for terror? Gray was for without.

Someone knocked gently on her door and she knew who it was. "Yeah?" she asked, without turning around.

"I'm sorry, Zoe," her dad said. "And I'm sure your mother is, too. But it'll be okay. You'll be okay, I promise."

"Okay," she answered.

"Are you okay now?" he asked.

"It's just—I've got a lot of reading, and the math is hard, so—"

"If you want help?"

"If I can't figure it out on my own, I'll . . ."

"I'll leave you to it then," his voice said, and she heard the door closing softly.

After a while, she turned on her computer and did pull up a sudoku, which she solved easily. She could almost feel her brain flicking through numbers, this, no that, yes, next? Focusing on filling in the squares steadied her; she could feel it happening. By the end of the game, she was ready for math problems. She opened her math folder to the assigned page.

And an envelope fell out.

An envelope? In her math folder?

An envelope with just her name on it in block capitals.

ZOE PRINZ

It was pretty fancy, for a fifth-grade birthday party invitation, but she was so separated from her friends, how would she know what to expect? She opened the envelope, wondering whose parents used fancy envelopes like this for a kids' party. Maybe Lucy? Lucy always had the newest in sneakers and stylish tops.

But it wasn't a party invitation. There were just a couple of scraps of gray tissue paper inside, plus a message that could be for anybody: ONE WISH AT A TIME. One for each sheet of tissue? That was simple enough, and so was WHISPER IT TO ME. But BE WISE could mean anything. Don't waste a wish, for one thing, on anything silly like— What would be a silly wish? One that asked for a lifetime supply of peanut-butter cups, maybe. Although knowing you could always have a peanut-butter cup would be pretty terrific. Better would be wishing for something like a money tree, which would mean you could always buy your own candy, along with anything else you wanted, a swimming pool, a trip to Disney World, or a second honeymoon cruise for her parents, around the world maybe—Zoe laughed to herself. Around the world would take a long time, so Mrs. Chester and Baxter would have to move into their house, and think of how happy Connor would be about that.

Assuming this was real magic, which Zoe didn't believe in any more than she believed in Santa Claus or Bigfoot.

Somebody in her class had put it into her math folder. Somebody with a really creative imagination. She started to wonder who, beginning with J'Shaun who never volunteered answers but always knew them when a teacher called on him. Because magic was impossible, and magician's tricks were only tricks, even if you couldn't figure them out.

Although, if there was magic around? And if a bit of it had fallen into her hands? And if she tried it?

Because, *What if?*

Because besides, nobody but her would know what a dimwit she'd been.

Also because she knew what she'd wish for if she believed in magic and had been given a genuine magic wish.

If she wished it and it didn't come true, there was nothing lost, was there? But if she wished it and it happened, even if it had nothing to do with wishing, that would be a good thing. Wouldn't it? She didn't know about WISE, but it wasn't a silly wish, or greedy—unless it was selfish? But it wasn't just for her. It was for all of them, if it worked, so she took one of the thin rectangles and whispered into it, "I wish my parents would stop having these Ugly Fights."

Of course doing that did make her feel foolish, and

childish, too, except . . . The tissue disappeared. It was just gone. Faded or melted, and it happened so fast she didn't notice it was happening until it was done. When she looked for it, the notepaper, too, was gone, and the envelope with it.

Zoe didn't know what to think. Because what if—? Then, as if there was some danger of being caught doing something she'd been told not to, copying on a test, or kissing a boy— Although kissing she hadn't been told by anybody not to do, it was just that nobody did so it would mark you out and— And what was it about kissing anyway? Then, almost as if she was guilty of something, she tucked the remaining tissue into her math folder, deep in the pocket where she kept corrected homework sheets.

What if the wish came true and she never again had to hear her parents having an Ugly Fight, and neither did Connor? What if the wish was really magical? If it was, then she had a second one and she could wish for anything she wanted, to have her friends back or a wallet that never ran out of money or even to be a famous . . . something, painter or actress or even surgeon. If it was magic—which it couldn't be—Zoe knew better than to use it right away. She'd set it aside, for later, in case.

THREE

If it was magic at work, it was Aladdin-style magic, a magic carpet where you just say the word, just to see if it's real, and—whip, whap, whoosh—you're airborne, no time to pack or plan, just grabbing on to the fringed edge so you won't blow off.

Her parents stopped speaking to one another.

It took her a day or two to notice, and even then she turned to Connor to confirm it. She didn't want to upset him, so she couldn't ask him straight out. "What was it Mom was saying to Dad about summer camp?"

"I wasn't listening," he answered.

This told her that the opposite was true, but she wanted to be sure. "When was the last time you heard her say something to him?"

"They're not getting divorced," he told her.

"Would you mind if they did?" she asked him.

"Would we have to live somewhere else? Because my mobile is nailed into the ceiling."

"Things can be un-nailed, Connor."

"But I really like my teacher this year. Who would live with us?"

It wouldn't do any good if Connor got all worked up. "Don't be a baby," she told him.

"I'm not, I'm almost eight, and you're stupid to say that." He glared at her. Then, "Are they? Getting divorced."

"You have to ask them."

"No I don't."

On Friday, before their father had returned with the weekly groceries, they left the house with their mother. Mom gave them each five dollars and half an hour at the arcade, then took them to the Chinese restaurant for dinner. She let them have a full order of egg rolls apiece and asked to have anything they hadn't finished, including the rice, put into carryout containers for them to take home. When they got there the shopping bags were lined up on the counter, un-emptied except for frozen peas and orange juice and a quart of the chocolate ice cream Zoe and Connor loved. All Mom said was, "That wasn't on the list." She didn't seem surprised that the house was unoccupied, which was how they learned that their father had decided to move out. "Not everyone has the character to see things through," Mom said, explaining that she and Dad would be living apart for a while.

So they must have talked to one another at least enough to plan this, Zoe thought.

Saturday mornings Mom went to the gym and as usual it was Dad who kept an eye on the kids. That Saturday he arrived at the front door instead of just coming downstairs. "I'm at the Parkside Hotel," he told them. "You know where it is, right? Just for a couple of days."

"Then you're coming home?" Connor asked.

Zoe knew better.

"All TBD," Dad said, trying for a cheery voice. "Your mother needs to get away— Not from you kids, it's just me." He shrugged, offered a small smile, rubbed at his forehead. "For now, I'm going to rent a place, something furnished, as close as I can get to you. Because I'm not about to be cut off from you kids. You know that, right? Zoe? Connor? I'll always be here for you."

"And Mom," Connor added.

Dad looked quickly at Zoe, and she shrugged, offering her own small smile.

❑ ❑ ❑

"Are you kids doing okay?" both of her grandmothers asked, and both of them assured her, "We're here if you need to talk, you or Connor, we're here for you. We'll always be here for you," which might have meant that they thought their mom and dad might not take good enough care of Zoe and Connor, didn't it? Or maybe it didn't. How was Zoe supposed to know what they really thought? She didn't know herself what to think, or who to listen to. Mr. K was right about one thing, anyway; she wasn't about to take sides.

She didn't know what would happen next. She didn't know who she could talk to about it, either. Neither Mom nor Dad was a good idea. "She's already got a lawyer." "He needs a wake-up call." And Zoe no longer had a real friend. In fact, the only person she felt okay about being around was Connor, and he only wanted to talk about galaxies and science and the atmosphere on Venus. But Connor wasn't sucking his thumb and she wasn't sitting in the same room with Ugly Fighting, so Zoe didn't feel like complaining.

The house Dad rented was two stories, and on a street called Dahlia Circle, right next to the park. Two cul-de-sacs had been put there and the five houses on each were pretty much the same. "In spring, as soon as the weather gets nice? You'll have the whole park for a yard," he told them when he came to get them on Saturday morning for their first overnight with him. "Who's going to get first pick of bedrooms? After me, I mean. I already picked the biggest, too bad for you guys."

Sometimes Dad teased with his usual relaxed cheerfulness and sometimes he was sorry and apologetic. Mom acted sorry and cross. She talked about hiring somebody, a part-time housekeeper, since she had been left holding the baby.

"I'm not a baby," Connor objected, and Mom was immediately sorry.

"I know that, love, I didn't mean that kind of baby. It's just—my job keeps me busy. It takes a lot out of me. I want to have time to enjoy you guys."

"Maybe Mrs. Chester could do it?" Zoe wondered, and Connor pitched right in, "Because we have a fenced yard so Baxter would be safe."

"Sometimes I think you like Mrs. Chester better than me," Mom answered, but she was smiling. "Unfortunately for you, she has her own family so she is only available in the evenings, and we need someone who will take care of the grocery shopping, and get you to appointments and school stuff when I'm at work."

"That's Dad's job," Connor reminded her.

"You men certainly do stick together," Mom said.

"He wasn't saying it like that," Zoe said.

"Maybe not. Sorry again. I don't know. These days, I feel like I never know anything."

"Mommy? Don't be sad," Connor said, and wrapped his arms around her waist, which was as high as he could reach. "Isn't it going to be all right?"

"I have no idea what it's going to be," Mom said.

Zoe could sympathize with that. Even if, at the same time, it wasn't going to be Ugly Fights, and she was glad about that.

The plan was for Zoe and Connor to live in their own home, where they had their own rooms, as usual. Dad had almost exactly the same hours they did, so he was the one who was home with them after school, to do whatever driving needed doing and get dinner started. Mom called before she left work so Dad could be gone before she arrived but the kids wouldn't spend more than a few minutes alone and unsupervised. If she was going to be late, Dad stayed to eat with them. They went to Dad's new house for Saturday nights, so each parent had a day to themselves. They were given small overnight suitcases, as if this was some kind of a present-giving occasion.

Then Mom had a convention, and had to be away for a whole school week because the meetings were in Ireland, overseas, so Dad moved back into the house and they had better lunches. They were going to talk to Mom on the phone every night at six, because of her schedule and the time difference. This worked for the first two nights. Zoe and Connor got ten minutes apiece to report to Mom about how they were feeling, if they were having fun with Dad, and what happened at school. She asked what they had for supper, because she kept forgetting that they ate at six thirty, and after three nights she forgot about making the call. Dad suggested, "You know how important her job is."

"More important than me?" Connor asked.

"Do you want me to text her?" Dad offered.

They all knew that was a bad idea.

"It's spetty-hag for supper," Dad said, reminding them of what Zoe had called spaghetti before she could really talk.

"With meatballs?" Connor asked.

"If there are any left," Dad answered, as he opened the freezer. After dinner, because all three of them had finished whatever homework needed to be done for the next day, they sat in a row on the sofa, Dad in the middle, to watch *Coco*.

The only thing missing was Mom.

Mom got home Friday, after dinner. With his suitcase standing ready beside the door, Dad waited for her to actually walk in, because with rush-hour traffic you couldn't tell how long the drive from the airport would take. "They missed talking to you when you stopped calling," was all he said to her, but she was so glad to see them she didn't bother fighting back. They spent that whole weekend at home, because she'd missed them. She'd brought both of them a special Irish sweater. "For next winter when it's cold, or rainy weather. It's the kind Irish fishermen wear." She slept in Saturday morning but in the afternoon they all went to the new Spiderman movie and had a pizza dinner, in the pizzeria instead of carrying it home which meant that the pizza was fresh and hot and really good. On Sunday, she went over their homework pages with them, which was usually Dad's job but Mom liked doing it, too. She talked with Connor about the possibility of other sentient beings in the galaxy, and why she, for one, didn't think Venus would be a good planet for a colony. She talked with Zoe about school, her classes and if she liked learning things, and if Zoe would be playing softball this spring because on a softball team she might find a new group of friends. They played a dozen or more games of Rat-a-Tat Cat, and Mom won most of them.

The only thing missing was Dad.

Then it was spring, and warm. They could spend more time outside, which meant being near the park made Dahlia Circle a great place to live. The park was huge, with not only wide grassy green lawns all around it but also concrete sidewalks, perfect for Rollerblading, some level and straight, some with inclines, some with curves, all wide enough for two people to skate side by side, as Zoe and her father discovered, because he decided to get fit and bought himself a set of blades, so they could skate together on weekends. Then it turned out that there was another space-crazy boy living two houses down, and his father was an actual scientist. A genuine biologist who worked in a research laboratory, doing experiments to discover better food for farm animals to eat, especially cows, so they wouldn't add so many pollutants into the environment. Methane from cows' farts, for example. Connor and Jimmy snickered happily every time they said that, but mostly Jimmy was interested in scientific talk about the planet Jupiter. The two boys argued seriously and for hours about the likelihood of intelligent life on their favorite planets; Jimmy thought that several moons gave Jupiter the advantage, but Connor argued that Venus, being closer to Earth, had temperature ranges that were much closer to what had resulted in human life on Earth. They argued surfaces and atmospheres and what forms of life either planet might maintain. Jimmy didn't go to their school. He was in a special magnet school for kids who liked science and were already good at it. Dad promised that he and Mom would look into the school for Connor.

There were no kids close to Zoe's age on Dahlia Circle, although because of the lighter traffic she could cross streets and hang out with a couple of girls in her class who lived just off Garden Street. On Dahlia Circle there were just teenaged sisters, already in high school, and Jimmy and his little brother, and the woman directly across the street who had three children already but was going to have another baby. "She's due any day now," her father told her. "You could find work as a mother's helper, maybe. Would you like that, Zoe?"

Actually, what Zoe liked best was the park, where she and her father zoomed around on Rollerblades, or they threw a Frisbee back and forth and talked, about everything, her school and his, work and Connor, books, the news, what to eat for supper . . . everything except her mother. There was the occasional comment, like "Your mother likes her clothes stylish" or "It's important to learn how to stand up for yourself, your mother's right about that." Over suppers they all looked into how a wind farm works, and discussed dishes her father had found online, meals from all around the world, fancy or plain didn't matter. Zoe didn't exactly make new friends at the park, but there were regular families to wave at, with little kids, and a pair of brothers, one younger than Zoe, one older, who came every day with a dalmatian dog they'd taught to play Frisbee with them. After a couple of weeks, Zoe and her father called, "Hey," to the boys, who called back a hello. After a while, they sometimes, all four, plus Sandman, threw the Frisbee together—except for Sandman, who of course could only fetch.

There was a pond in the park with a fountain shooting out water at its center for when the weather turned hot, and flowers in colorful patches around statues, a dog park, and a quarter-mile cinder track, and two playgrounds—a fenced-in one for little kids with smaller swings and a merry-go-round and a climbing gym made of wood, with a slide that ended up in a soft bed of wood chips, as well as one for older kids with soft rubber flooring under swings and rings, zip lines, and a climbing wall. A couple of Saturday afternoons, Dad had work or wanted to watch football, so Zoe went on her own to the park. She skated by herself, seeing all the people, in couples or groups or families, and noticed the way gray squirrels dashed from the safety of one tree to the safety of the next. She smelled newly mown grass and freshly turned flower beds that had just been rained on and enjoyed being alone with her own thoughts.

It was certainly easier to enjoy things now that she was no longer stuck in a house with two angry people, fighting ugly. It was so easy that at first she didn't notice the way they were now unhappy in new ways. She was so accustomed to seeing their anger that she didn't really register the way Mom was now complaining about how her job didn't fulfill her, or that Dad had started grumbling about how little the Board of Education paid the people who had the responsibility for taking care of children all day long while their parents had jobs that paid good salaries. She didn't even think it was odd how glad their parents were to see them at the beginnings of their visiting times, and relieved, too, when Zoe followed Connor in, both of them pulling their suitcases behind them. It was as if their parents were afraid they wouldn't actually arrive. "What would you like to do?" they asked, as if without Zoe and Connor they had nothing to interest them. Even though both had jobs, and friends, and chores to be done in their separate houses.

She wasn't sure what her parents were feeling. They never said they were happy, now, or even happier having separate houses. But they hadn't ever said they weren't happy, before, had they? Could they have enjoyed the fighting? But Zoe felt so much better, and Connor—except for sometimes complaining about having to leave his mobile and posters behind when he went to Dad's—no longer excused himself from the dinner table, not in either house, and didn't hide out in his room all the time. All her parents said about being separated was to explain about the other one. "Your mother wants." "Your father thinks." It was as if they each wanted the other to be at fault. Zoe was tempted to tell them that in fact it was her fault, since she'd made the wish.

Then, at the end of April, with only a few more

weeks to go before summer vacation, when they had settled into this new way of living, she and Connor were told that there would be a change: "Your mother feels like she doesn't have enough free time with you two," Dad told them. Mom's version was, "Your father wants weekends free." The new plan was for Zoe and Connor to spend a week at a time in one house or the other, changing homes on Wednesdays. They needed to be sure to pack up the right school supplies, and any special outfits or equipment, to take to school on Wednesday. During the week away, the other parent—the absent one—wasn't supposed to call very often, and interrupt the host parent's time with them. Dad found duplicates of Connor's posters and they picked out a new mobile of the planets, actually more detailed than the one Connor had had hanging from his ceiling at home.

Except, what was home now?

Then, more than halfway through May, with summer coming up and Dad having a summer job because he needed the money, with Connor's day camp being at the park and Zoe's arts and crafts camp at the high school, the whole family met up together at the Chinese restaurant. "Neutral ground," Mom said and Dad didn't argue.

"Your mother thinks things will run more smoothly for you kids if one of you lives full time with me and the other with her. Although there will be sleepovers, I'm not giving either of you up."

"Your father's summer schedule means he can't manage two children, not even three days a week. It goes without saying that I feel the same about sleepovers, you'll always have your room in my house."

Connor looked at Zoe. Zoe looked at Connor. "When?" she asked them. "When would this happen?"

"Are you getting divorced?" Connor asked.

"Who decides who goes where?" Zoe asked.

"I have to go to the bathroom," said Connor.

"Why don't you kids take a day or two to think which would work best for you?" Mom suggested.

"Would you mind so much if we did this? Connor? Zoe?" Dad asked. "Would it be so bad?"

"I'd like the time to think about it," Zoe told them both, and she got up from the table. "Connor would, too," she added, although she didn't actually know that. "I have to go to the bathroom, too."

Because this was terrible. Absolutely, perfectly, awfully terrible. This was literally breaking her family in half. Zoe felt as if she was out in the middle of a lake and had suddenly forgotten how to swim, splashing and gasping for breath with no lifeguard around.

She wished she'd never made that wish.

But couldn't she use the second wish to undo the first? That's if it really was magic.

But what if it wasn't?

FOUR

Because Zoe and Connor were at their mother's that week, they couldn't go to the park to have a private conversation. Luckily for them, Mom had a big case to work on, so she was glued to her computer. As soon as they got home, Zoe and Connor headed for their rooms. "What's with you two?" Mom asked. "It's a lovely afternoon, you should be outside—throwing a Frisbee? I wish I didn't have to work, but if we want to see a movie tomorrow, this has to get done today."

Connor mumbled something about "library book" but Zoe stopped to explain. "I have a report comparing Native American societies, the nomadic Plains tribes with the Pueblo tribes of the Southwest. It's due at the end of next week, and I'd really like to see a movie tomorrow so . . ."

"It's good to be serious about school, Zoe, and don't let anyone tell you different," Mom answered as she picked up her computer case from the hall table.

Zoe followed Connor into his bedroom and shut the door behind her. "That explains why they took us out for lunch," she said, stretching out on his twin bed. "Both of them together, I mean."

For once, Connor wasn't either seated on the floor in front of his bookcase, reading some planet book, or at his desk drawing pictures of what a sentient being who was native to the atmosphere on Venus might look like. For once, he was standing. Just standing there, at the foot of his own bed. For once, Connor looked right straight at her to tell her what he was thinking: "I want to be the one who lives with Dad."

Zoe was shocked.

Not shocked that Dad would be Connor's choice, and not that she would be brokenhearted to be the one to live with Mom. She was shocked that Connor was grabbing for what he wanted. Connor never grabbed. He wanted, and hoped, and waited, but he didn't just take.

What was happening to her brother?

Was it good or bad, this change in him?

Did it have to do with the way their family had broken apart?

Was all this her fault, too?

"Shouldn't the boys live together?" Connor asked.

"Dad's not a boy." She couldn't think of anything else to say.

"You know what I mean," Connor insisted, and he was right.

"Does that mean you want them to get divorced?" she wondered. "Do you think they will?"

Connor shrugged. "What I want doesn't matter to them. Or you, what you want."

"I just wanted them to stop fighting."

"So you got your wish," he pointed out, "and mine is to be the one that lives with Dad."

"Why?" she asked, starting to get over her surprise at actually talking with her galaxy-crazed little brother. "Do you like him better?"

"I like both of them the same," Connor told her. "Don't you?"

She didn't have to think about that. "Yes. So why?"

"Jimmy's my friend."

"You have other friends, Kieran and Seymour, Bobby, sometimes you play with Jenny and Inge, Chet and Wes and—"

"You know what I mean," Connor told her again, and he was right again. "I never have to explain things to Jimmy. Or pretend either."

Zoe remembered what it felt like to have friends like

that. She didn't blame Connor, not one bit. She knew she'd be all right, living with her mother. They both liked being busy and two females were a better natural fit. She knew puberty was going to happen to her and wouldn't another female be better able to explain it to her? And know how to talk to her about it? But— "I'd rather be a family, all four of us." As soon as she said it, she understood how true that was. "Just, without them fighting."

"If wishes were horses," Connor answered with a smile, because it was what Grammy always said.

"Beggars would ride," she finished, smiling back, thinking of their grandparents in their house down in Alabama with two wide porches to catch any summer breeze, only two blocks from the beach, where she and Connor spent weeks of summer, until their parents came to pick them up.

"If they get divorced and I live with Dad, can you still come to Alabama?" Connor asked. "Do grand-parents get divorced from the family, too?"

"I don't know," Zoe said. She didn't, and she hadn't when she made the wish. She'd just made it, without any idea what might happen to make it come true. "Do you want us to live in separate places?" she asked her brother. "You and me."

"If I have to," he said. "I'd get used to it I guess. Wouldn't you?"

"Probably, but—"

"I don't like changing every Wednesday, the different buses, and taking a suitcase to school. Nobody else does that. All the other kids with divorced parents only live in one place, and they visit the other parent. They don't live with both in two different places."

"I don't think Mom would like almost never seeing you. Or Dad, either, he wouldn't like not to see me very much."

Connor's eyes got wide. "Could that happen?"

"I don't know," Zoe said, again.

This was the most grown-up conversation she'd ever had with her brother and she couldn't help noticing that she kept having to say I don't know.

"What should we do, Zoe?" her brother asked.

He didn't know that the last time Zoe had "done something" it had caused all their present problems. She wasn't the one to ask. She didn't want to say I don't know again, so she didn't say anything. She chewed on her lip.

After a while, "I guess, a week at a time isn't that bad," Connor said. "I don't want to belong to just one or the other of them."

"Do we belong to them?" Zoe asked. Since she was feeling like she didn't know anything, she hoped maybe her brother—her galaxy-crazed little brother—could tell her how to understand what she had already done.

"Sort of. If you think about it. It's what happens when you're somebody's kid, they make the rules, and the decisions, because they have to take care of you, because they're your parents."

Zoe stopped chewing her lip and stared.

"What? What's wrong with that? It's true and you know it. That's what's so bad about divorce. When parents get divorced, kids get divorced too."

Zoe kept staring.

"Zoe," Connor protested. "You're acting creepy."

This sounded like the little brother she was used to. "Oh, sorry. But—I was just thinking— Because what you just said? You're getting smarter, Connor."

"What does that mean?"

A little-boy answer. Or a little-brother don't-pester-me answer. He didn't want to think about it. "I think you might be," she warned him.

What would happen if she told him about the wishes? The one she'd made and the one she had left.

Except she was the one they'd been given to. Were they supposed to be secret?

Anyway, Connor wouldn't believe in magic.

"Do you remember when you found out there was no Santa Claus?" she asked him.

"I always knew that," her brother answered. He wasn't interested in the question. He had something else on his mind. "We should make a list, pros and cons, that's the way a scientist would do it." He sat at his desk, took a sheet of paper out of the drawer, and picked up a pencil. PRO he wrote, then, halfway down the page, CON.

Why not go along with him? It would give him something to do while she was trying to figure out whether or not to confide in him. Because she did have one wish left. Maybe it could fix things. Maybe even Connor would have a good idea for it, something that wouldn't backfire the way the first wish had.

"Jimmy." Connor began his list of pros for Dad's house. "Dad plays cards with us, he likes that. But he doesn't have a smart TV." He put smart TV at the top of Mom's pros.

Zoe didn't have a Jimmy on her list, pro or con. "Mom's got the good job," she said. "Write that down, Connor, and the Prius, and good health insurance. It's going to cover your braces, remember? And braces are really expensive."

"Would I have to have a new doctor if I'm living with Dad?"

"I don't know. With Mom, we don't have to worry about money, or economizing. Mom earns more. But the park is next to Dad's."

"And Dad's a good cook."

A definite pro.

"Mom likes eating out. And she takes us to movies."

"She'd still help out paying for us, wouldn't she? For whoever wasn't living with her," Connor asked.

"I think that depends on the deal they make between them."

A deal made between parents about the kids. Zoe wondered if Connor was thinking the same thing. Both of them were silent. Zoe didn't know about her brother, but what she was now thinking about was how neither one of them had any say. Nobody was asking them or telling them anything. Nobody was including them in the decisions. The deal.

"They each give us our own bedrooms," Connor pointed out.

"So that's the same. Mom hates Clue, and fantasy games, even Dragonwood. She doesn't even like Uno."

"She likes crossword puzzles and Bananagrams. I really like playing Scrabble with her. She doesn't give me any help with words so when I have a good word it's all mine," Connor said.

"Dad talks to me the same way he talks to grown-ups," Zoe realized.

"Me, too."

"And I like Scrabble, too. Not as much as Clue, because Clue makes you think. If you want to win."

"Don't you like our Uno games with Dad? Just because it's not challenging doesn't mean it's not just as much fun, Zoe."

"There are different kinds of fun, Connor, and I prefer the kind that makes you think."

"Can't I want both of them together? I know I'm not going to get both—I do know that—but they asked us what we wanted and both *is* what I want."

For a minute, Zoe was confused. "You mean both Mom and Dad?"

"I know that's impossible. Don't worry, Zoe, I do know that."

But Zoe knew more. She knew something Connor didn't. That is, if it was real magic, she did. She wondered if her brother— But he was her galaxy-crazed little brother; what could he know that she didn't? She was three years older, and the kind of person who paid attention to what was right there, around her, not distant planets you couldn't know anything about because of all the clouds around them.

Except, she couldn't think of the smart thing to do here, right here right now, and maybe Connor could. Besides, it was as important to him as it was to her, wasn't it?

Besides besides, it wasn't a smart thing she was trying to think of. The instructions said wise— BE WISE—and she'd failed at that the first time. Maybe a galaxy-crazed little boy could figure out something better.

Zoe took a deep breath. "Connor, you know how magic isn't real? And there's no such thing as magic wishes?"

"What does that—" he started to ask, but she interrupted him.

"Back last winter," she began the story, starting with how unhappy the Ugly Fighting made her. "And them, too, they must have been unhappy, too. You remember the last one, don't you? The chicken parmesan supper? Although, you ran away to the bathroom."

"I really did have to go," Connor said. "So what?"

"That night . . . in my math folder? This sounds crazy I know but . . . There was an envelope for me, with my name but no address, and inside? You'll think I'm making it up, Connor, but I'm not, I promise," she said, looking right into his listening face. "Inside, there were two pieces of tissue paper, little, the size of playing cards, and there were instructions. It said they were wishes, and I needed to whisper my wish into one, and it said I should be wise."

She gave him a few seconds to object, but he didn't. Neither did he look like someone who has been given a good explanation. She continued.

"I made a wish," she told him. "I wished that they'd stop fighting like that. And they did. Right away the next morning. They stopped talking to one another at all, remember? So my wish came true."

"I remember it was after that we went to the arcade and out to supper and when we got back home, Dad was gone. It was a Friday."

Zoe nodded.

"And you think it was your wish coming true?" Connor asked.

She nodded.

"You know better," he told her. "You know magic doesn't make things happen. That's what science can do, once things have been figured out. Science is what tells you how things happen."

"I know," she admitted. "Except—"

"What did you do with the note?" he asked. "And

the wishes, once you'd used them? They'd be proof. Do you have proof?"

"The note disappeared as soon as I read it. And the envelope had already disappeared. The wish paper, too, after. They just . . . melted away into air."

Connor shook his head. "See, Zoe, that can't happen. There'll be some explanation, like invisible ink. Matter doesn't just disappear."

"But it did. I'm not lying."

Connor looked at his list of pros and cons. Then he stood up and walked to his dresser. Then he crossed the room to sit down on his own bed. He was thinking.

Zoe watched him, waiting.

After a while, "I don't believe it."

Zoe nodded.

"It's—totally unscientific."

"But you believe there is intelligent life on another planet," she pointed out. "A planet nobody scientific says could support life."

"I know, but maybe there could be," he argued. "It's not entirely impossible. There are cosmic rays, somebody could be sending out cosmic rays. Or have some way of being alive that's adapted to the environment on Venus. They way all life on Earth is adapted to our environment."

"That's all I'm saying," Zoe answered. "Not entirely impossible. I don't even know what I actually believe about it. I just know that I made a wish and the fights stopped."

Connor nodded and studied the hands he spread out over his bony knees. Then he had an idea. "If you got two wishes? Where's the other one? Can you show it to me? Seeing is believing," he told her.

Something else their Grammy liked to say.

"Wait here," she told him, and went to get her math folder. They were in this together now, sister and brother, Zoe and Connor.

FIVE

Zoe sat on the bed beside her brother and opened the folder. For a hopeful minute—unless it was the opposite of hopeful?—she thought she might not find the wish, but there it was, in among the corrected papers. She held it out to Connor.

He didn't try to touch it.

"See?"

"Yeah."

"So do you believe me now?"

Connor thought. "Maybe," he decided. "If you had two more of them, we could try a practice one. Just to be sure."

Zoe was about to point out that she'd done that, except she couldn't be sure she had actually caused her parents to split up. She hoped she hadn't, but the split sure meant that her wish had been granted.

"We could wish for a dog!" Connor realized. "I'd like a dog, and so would you. Like Baxter."

Zoe smiled, because this was such a little-kid wish.

"But we would like it," Connor insisted, "and maybe Mom and Dad would, too, and things would get back to normal because of the dog."

"The instructions said the wish should be wise," Zoe told him.

"Where are they, anyway?"

"They disappeared. I told you."

"Don't you want a dog?" Connor insisted. "That's my idea for the wish, and you just said I'm getting smarter."

But it's my wish, Zoe thought.

Right away she knew better. Her wishing had changed Connor's life, too, so it didn't belong only to her. It belonged to both of them, together.

"In science," Connor told her, "you have an idea and you think of ways to check it. Test it. That's what experiments are, and you write down the results to see if they match your idea."

"But we only have one wish so we can't experiment," Zoe reminded him.

"I guess. But if it's not a dog— What is our idea?"

That was the right question. It made sense.

"Do we want them to get back together? Even if they went back to fighting like that?" she asked.

Connor didn't answer right away. Eventually, he decided. "I don't think so. Not really. Do you?"

"I hated the fighting. At least this way they don't fight. But do you think they're serious about splitting us up? Each of them taking one of us?"

"Wouldn't you like being with Mom?"

"I'd be okay with either one of them," she said, being honest. "I don't have a Jimmy at either place."

"They should never have gotten married," Connor announced.

"They must have been in love. Don't you think?"

"People don't get married unless they're in love," Connor said. "Do they?"

"How would I know?" Zoe demanded.

Connor giggled, and the silliness of two kids talking about why grown-ups get married struck Zoe, too. "Okay," she said, when she'd gotten serious again. "Okay, maybe they were. So what? They aren't now."

"But we can wish they get back in love again? Wish for that, Zoe. At least things would get back to normal."

"Normal was the Ugly Fights," she pointed out. "Normal didn't have Jimmy."

"I mean normal before that. That's my idea anyway and if we make the wish and it comes true, that's our experiment being a success. I can have playdates with Jimmy, can't I?"

Zoe thought about what WISE was. It wasn't what she did with her first wish, not thinking ahead to what could be. She said, "If normal before turned into fighting, who's to say that's not just going to happen all over again. They're still the same people."

"Oh." Connor fell silent. She was about to apologize for shooting down his idea when he had a question. "Do you know when it started? The not being in love. The fighting."

Zoe shook her head. "All I know is we were all unhappy. Them included."

"I wasn't," Connor said.

Maybe he'd forgotten how he hid in the bathroom and hid in his room, hid in his drawings of alien lifeforms. Maybe he was pretending it never happened. She wondered if she should remind him, and decided not to.

"We both were," she announced. "You know that, Connor," she told him.

He nodded. "Do you think that if you hadn't made that wish we'd still be a whole family?"

"If it's magic. If the magic is real. I guess."

She looked down at the flimsy paper she held in

her right hand. It didn't look one bit magical—no sparkles, no twinkles, no waving in an invisible breeze or changing colors. So maybe it wasn't and it didn't make any difference what she used the wish for so she should go ahead and wish for a dog, just in case, and give her brother what he wanted so at least one of them could be happy?

As soon as she thought the word, she could see the idea, standing there right in front of her, waiting to be noticed.

"What if," she began, and went slowly on, carefully speaking out loud and not raising her right hand from her lap. "What if we wish that all of us are happy?"

"Then Dad would come back home?"

"I don't know. Happy isn't the same as excited, or no longer angry. But I guess he might. You could still be friends with Jimmy even if you don't live on his street."

"Would being happy keep them from fighting?" Connor wondered.

Zoe kept it honest. "Maybe. For sure there wouldn't be any more Ugly Fights."

"Then it's a good wish to try, Zoe. Anyway, that's my decision," Connor told her.

Right away, however, he had doubts. "What about

us? Will we still have to pick who to live with? If they don't get back together, can I pick you?"

This was a new way of looking at it. Zoe wouldn't mind living with either one of her parents, because she loved them both, and probably it was the same for Connor, except for Jimmy. The only thing that would make her un-happy with any arrangement was not having Connor there with her, whichever house she was living in. She didn't understand why, but if she wanted to be happy she needed her galaxy-crazed little brother, living with her, full time.

She hadn't known that before. But it didn't really surprise her. And it sounded like Connor felt the same.

"I want to try that for the wish," she told him. "I want to wish that we stay together, you and me. Whatever they decide to do."

Connor was staring at her, curious, and a little afraid. "Can I watch? Will it work?"

Zoe laughed. "We'll find out," and she raised the tissue paper to her lips and made her wish. When the paper just disappeared from between her fingers, she laughed again, at the expression on her brother's face.

"Wow," said Connor, his eyes wide with the wonder of it.

"Exactly," Zoe agreed.

THE DOG

ONE

Casey had no need to hurry home because there was nobody waiting there for her. Besides, the dogs on Daisy Lane already expected her. They came to their fences to meet her as she crisscrossed from one side of the street to another, saying hello, scratching gently, patting their heads. Over the two weeks she'd been walking to and from the school bus, she had named each of the dogs.

The German shepherd lived just off Garden Street. "Hello Fritz," she greeted him. He stuck his nose as far as it would go through the chain-link fence. She reached her fingers out and stroked it. "It's Friday tomorrow," she told him. "The end of the second-to-last week of school." He wagged his tail at this news.

Across the street, the white toy poodle yapped at her from behind a screened window. She waved and wondered: no voice silenced little Henri and there was no fence around the grassy lawn. How did he get his exercise? When summer vacation began, maybe she'd see.

"Hello, hello, yes, hello Spot." Casey was almost the same height as the head of the excited, brightly white and black dalmatian, who stood on his hind legs at his high fence. Spot wasn't exactly an original name, but she couldn't think of a better one. He licked her hand and grunted to say hello back.

"Going to the park today?" She pulled gently on his ear the way she'd read that dogs liked. Late in the afternoons, this dog was walked by two boys, brothers, she guessed. The bigger held the leash; the smaller carried a Frisbee.

She went by a few fenceless and dogless yards before she got to the picket fence where Good Dog was waiting for her. He was a medium-small dog, with short brown poodle curls and the square chest of a cocker spaniel. His stub of a tail wagged busily. Good Dog was her favorite. She gave him extra time, morning and afternoon, setting her backpack down and crouching to put her fingers through the pickets of his fence and scratch under his chin.

"You're a good dog."

He was glad to hear that.

"Such a good dog," she said, in a lullaby voice, and

his tail wagged double time. If it rained, which it didn't often in late spring, he was the only dog left outside. All Casey knew about Good Dog's owner was that he drove a little red Mini-Minor, left early, returned late, and wasn't often around on weekends. She had never seen him. Maybe, once summer started, that would change.

"Having a good day?" she asked, then told him, "I didn't, really, but it wasn't bad either, so that's good enough."

Good Dog's tail kept wagging and he licked her fingers. He agreed.

The corgi who lived next door to Good Dog barked then, one sharp sound, "Me! My turn!"

"Uh-oh." Casey laughed, giving Good Dog a final gentle pull on one of his folded-over ears. "Gotta go."

"You're pretty impatient, Taffy," she scolded, bending over a matching picket fence to stroke the corgi's long, soft fur, from the top of his head to as far down his back as she could reach. "It's almost Friday," she told him, "almost the weekend."

He nudged her hand with his cold nose. "More!"

Casey laughed again. "You're bossy, too."

Her laughter was echoed from a window in the second story of Taffy's house. A woman, or maybe it was a girl, looked down at her. She had long dark hair and dark skin and the kind of laugh that was as fat and friendly as a donut. She was looking right at Casey.

Casey straightened up. She picked up her backpack.

"Her name's Lizzie." It was the woman's voice.

"Oh. Sorry," Casey called back, embarrassed to have been caught.

As she turned to walk away, the woman added, "After the queen. Of England. Because she always has corgis."

Casey raised a hand in a small goodbye wave and almost ran the rest of the way, her cheeks burning.

Home was a one-story rectangle with two bedrooms and a bathroom making up half of it. The rest was one long room that combined their kitchen, eating, and study areas. Casey stopped at the door to pull the long chain that held her house key out from under her T-shirt.

From the first time she'd done this, Casey's heart always lifted like a helium balloon rising into the air when she unlocked the door into their own house. Not someone else's house they were house-sitting for a weekend or a week or a month, which—however nice it was and however good the school district was—they knew they would soon leave.

Also this house was not their usual room-with-kitchenette at the Desert View Motel, which would have been better named the Gas Station View now that the city had eaten up all the nearby scrublands. Here on Daisy Lane, Casey had her own key for the door to their own house. Around this house were other streets lined with houses, not strip malls. Casey hadn't gone beyond her own block but even there, walking to and from the school bus stop or just sitting on the doorstep as she had done a couple of times, in these first days in their own house, she could tell that she was living in a neighborhood that had all kinds of people of all ages. There were bigger houses than theirs, which was the smallest, and she hadn't seen any other car as faded as their old, extra safe Volvo, but being poor wasn't the kind of thing that bothered Casey and her mother. Things were on the upswing, Faye said. It might not have happened until she was almost at the end of fifth grade, but now Casey was enrolled in a school where she would stay longer than a week or a month. Faye was as pleased as her daughter about this. "That's step one checked off," she said. "It was the hardest part of the plan to get done and now it's behind us."

The plan was like a map that Faye could look at to be sure she was going in the right direction at the right speed. She planned to earn a double college degree, with majors in both business and computer studies, which would enable her to get a good job. Casey admired her mother's ability to make such an ambitious plan and stick to it. Her part of the plan was to not get in her mother's way, if she could help it, which—except for being there, being her daughter and a child—she mostly could. "Your mom's pretty fierce," was what Paco said, and Casey was proud to agree.

Before she even stepped all the way through the door, the phone rang. Faye's regular call. "Home okay?"

"I am." Their phone hung on the wall beside the door so Casey looked out at their street while they talked.

"I left you a note on the refrigerator."

"I see it." Not that anything much was going on out there.

"I'll be home not long after five."

"Okay." Casey could hear restaurant noises in the background, the clatter of plates and voices calling orders to the cook. "Busy?"

"Not too. Enough. See you soon." And they hung up.

That was when Casey noticed an envelope. It lay at her feet, just below the slot in the door for mail.

The envelope had her name on it. But who would write to her?

There was no address, only her name. In dark block capital letters.

CASEY HOOPER

This was very strange, and maybe strange enough to be scary. Her fingers holding the envelope suddenly felt stiff. Should she call her mother? Interrupt her at work? It could be nothing, couldn't it?

Casey dropped the envelope on the table and took down her mother's note from the refrigerator. "Lentil soup for supper. Check slow cooker. Biscuits in freezer. Sweep floor of big room."

She took four biscuits out of the bag in the freezer and put them on the counter to thaw. She checked that the slow cooker light was on and got the broom out of the closet.

The envelope lay on the table, trying to make her look at it.

Just her name was on it. No address. Sweep sweep. But it had been delivered to her house. Who knew her name and where she lived? Their landlord was in Massachusetts and had never met them; the house used to belong to his aunt. Sweep sweep, question, question, sweep sweep. It was strange. Was it someone creepy? Strange and scary? Sweep, sweep. Should she wait for Faye?

Get a grip, Casey told herself. You are eleven years old, old enough to come home from school to an empty house. It's only an envelope. She put the broom away, poured a glass of milk, got a grip, and took her usual seat at the table. From there, she could look out the door into a clear blue sky where only a couple of fat white clouds floated lazily. Nothing at all strange about that. Nothing to worry about.

Casey picked up the envelope, which had no return address, and no stamp either. She took a big drink of milk and pulled the back flap open.

So far, all normal.

Inside, a piece of heavy, expensive-looking paper was folded in half. She unfolded it, and two pieces of gray tissue paper slid onto the table. They were the size of playing cards, and blank.

Not normal, but not scary either. Still okay.

There was a typed message on the paper. It wasn't threatening. It wasn't full of hate. It wasn't even personal. There was no *Dear Casey*, and no signature. So, only strange, and only maybe creepy.

She read the words of the message:

ONE WISH AT A TIME

WHISPER IT TO ME

BE WISE

A dog, Casey thought.

Two pieces of flimsy paper, so two wishes? You whispered them to the pieces of paper?

A dog, she thought again, then, *No.*

Be wise? Because she had always wanted a dog but Faye had always said no.

But what if it was real magic?

Impossible. Even magicians were only performing tricks they'd learned how to do, and then rehearsed over and over; they used secret compartments and marked cards. Casey didn't believe in magic and she never had.

But what if she could wish for a dog and the wish came true? Some wishes did come true, even without magic.

And what was the harm in wishing, since magic wasn't real?

And even if it was real magic, if she magically got a dog and Faye hated it, she would have the other wish to unwish the first.

That was pretty wise, wasn't it?

Faye wouldn't be home for an hour, and why shouldn't Casey just try? Maybe after she'd reviewed the spelling words she'd gotten wrong on the test, and then—maybe—a wish?

Casey's attention returned to the tabletop. But the envelope was gone. The sheet of paper with instructions was gone, too. Only the two small pieces of gray tissue paper remained.

She was sure she hadn't thrown the envelope out, or the letter—not that she needed it. She remembered exactly what it said.

It couldn't be real magic, of course. Except, could it?

Impulsively, feeling almost mischievous and definitely more than a little foolish, Casey lifted one piece of gray tissue paper to her lips and whispered to it. "I wish I had a dog." She felt an embarrassed smile on her mouth as she was speaking the words, but that faded when the flimsy paper melted away from between her fingers.

She looked for the second piece of paper, half-expecting that it, too, would be gone. This could be some trick like invisible ink that only showed up when you heated it but disappeared as soon as it wasn't warm. But the second gray tissue-paper rectangle still lay on the tabletop.

Before anything weirder could happen, Casey picked it up, carefully. Tissue paper was easy to tear. She went to her desk, which was opposite to her mother's and facing away so they could both work undisturbed. She opened its one central drawer and put the gray tissue under her box of colored pencils. It wasn't that she was hiding it; it just needed to be kept out of sight. Real magic or some weird trick, either way Faye wouldn't like it. Faye might be young, only twenty-six-and-a-half, but she had her feet firmly on the ground and she planned to keep them there.

No amount of magic would make Faye welcome a dog. Dogs cost money, and they shed. Dogs made messes, and they had to be exercised. Casey was familiar with all the negative points of dogs. They barked, some bit, they could get you in trouble with landlords or neighbors. Nobody would hire a house sitter with a child *and* a dog. *We don't need the hassle,* Faye would say, and she would be right.

Remembering that made Casey feel bad. She almost wished she hadn't wished for a dog, and she was almost tempted to take the second tissue-paper card out of her drawer and unwish her first wish. Just in case.

Except, it was only a wish, and wishes didn't come true. Besides, it wasn't as if Faye didn't know she wanted a dog, so of course that's what she'd wish for, if she had a wish.

Casey settled at her desk and took out the practice spelling test. She was still there, still at work slowly writing words twenty-five times each, saying them out loud as she wrote then using them in three sentences, when Faye got home.

Faye was not carrying a puppy. Casey was not surprised.

TWO

No puppy in a cardboard box lay on their doorstep the next morning, Friday, when they left the house, and by the time Casey came home from school in the afternoon, she had pretty much forgotten about the tissue-paper wish. She zigzagged her usual way back and forth across the street, greeting dogs and feeling a little proud that now she knew Taffy's real name. "Here, Lizzie," she said softly, just to say it, even though the corgi was already waiting for her.

That afternoon, her chore was to sweep the bedrooms, after which she went outside to sit on the front step and look up and down Daisy Lane—her own street!—watching the passing cars and delivery vans. When a pedestrian came into sight, she slipped inside until the sidewalks were clear again.

Faye got home at five, parking the car on the road in front of their house. She went through the door Casey held open for her. After she drank a glass of water, she asked, "How was your day?"

"Okay," Casey told her. "Yours?"

"Oh, you know." Faye bent over to untie her sneakers and slip her feet out of them. She raised herself onto tiptoes a couple of times.

"Feet tired?"

"I'm okay."

Faye was always okay. Between classes and jobs and raising Casey, she didn't have the time to be anything else. *I know what I want and I know you've got to work for what you want*, was what Faye thought.

"Well," Faye said. She poured herself another glass of water. "I've got lab notes to recopy. You've got a book?"

Of course Casey had a book. On Fridays, she went to the library of whatever school she was attending to check out four or five of them. Faye had learned online that kids who read for thirty or forty minutes every day scored in the ninetieth percentile on standardized tests. Not just language arts tests, and not necessarily including math, but as a rule. So regular daily reading for Casey became part of the plan.

Casey set her books out in a row on her desk and looked at the spines, making up her mind. Behind her, Faye opened the notebook she carried to the twice-a-week biology lectures, the once-a-week two-and-a-half-hour lab, and the Sunday afternoon study group. Then she took out the notebook she kept in her desk, into which she recopied lecture notes and lab experiments. The required biology course was hard work for Faye.

Faye worked hard at learning. She also worked hard at house-sitting or waiting tables or restacking super-market shelves or delivering pizzas, but of all these jobs, learning was the hardest for her. "We're not nat-urally good at school, you and me," she told Casey, and as far as Casey could tell from her own experi-ence, that was true. She sat at her desk, her back to her mother, pulled a book from the row, and opened it. Faye wasn't the only one who knew how to work hard.

They had tuna-salad sandwiches for supper, with a banana or an apple for dessert. Faye washed the dishes and Casey dried. They did dishes once a day to save on dishwashing liquid. The Hoopers were good savers and because of that they had four months of living expenses set aside in a savings account, just in case. Faye had no intention of letting her daughter down.

After dinner they were both back at their desks when someone knocked on their door. Casey almost jumped out of her seat: nobody knew them on Daisy

Lane, and they didn't know anyone. It was Faye who answered, but Casey was right behind her, just in case.

Faye pulled the door open and Casey saw Good Dog right away, on the other side of the screen. He pressed his nose into it and she crouched down without thinking. "What are you doing here, Good Dog?"

His stubby tail wagged and his nose pushed harder against the screen.

"Your daughter," a voice said.

"What about my daughter?" Faye demanded in her don't-think-you-can-mess-with-me voice.

Casey got to her feet, to stand beside her mother.

A tall Black woman waited outside the screen door. She held a plastic grocery bag in one hand and a retractable leash in the other, to the end of which Good Dog was attached.

"There's no problem, it's just . . . I need a favor," the woman said. "I live down the street, in the second house? The little white one with a picket fence? The neighbors tell me that your daughter— Look, can I come in? It won't take long—I can't be long—but it'll be easier if . . ."

Faye hesitated.

"I'm harmless," the woman announced.

"So you say," Faye muttered, but she did take a step back, and so did Casey.

When they had entered, hovering just inside the door, Good Dog went right up to Casey, who bent down to pet his head, trying not to stare. This was the prettiest woman she had ever seen, tall and strong looking and with a face you just wanted to keep looking at. Really, she was beautiful, the first beautiful person Casey had ever seen. Her hair was cropped short and long silvery loops hung from her ears; her smile had a little sadness in it but her big dark eyes danced; she wore a denim jacket and black jeans and low-heeled red slingback shoes. Even in jeans, this woman looked fine enough to go to the ball and dance with the prince.

". . . a once-in-a-lifetime chance. You know how many of those come along? I passed one up, years ago, which is a mistake I won't repeat, I'll tell you. I just got the call ten minutes ago and the kennel has closed for the weekend. I thought your daughter could take Calvin in."

"I don't—" Faye began, but the woman cut her off.

"I'll pay, of course. There's an envelope with two hundred dollars in it in the bag with Calvin's bowls and dog food and blanket. Calvin is housebroken, and well past the chewing-on-things stage. I wouldn't bother you, except the neighbors— Have you met Eddy and Alba? They're expecting their first. It hasn't been an easy pregnancy but," she said, as if she feared, as Casey did, that Faye was about to hold open the screen door so she and her dog could leave, "they tell me your daughter likes dogs, and she's good with them."

"She does like them," Faye allowed.

Two hundred dollars was a lot of money. It was two of Faye's fat textbooks, for example, and maybe three if none of them was science. Five tanks of gas. Almost two weeks of groceries. Otherwise, Casey knew, Faye would have said no, right away.

"My daughter is only eleven," Faye pointed out. "And we don't—"

"I'm old enough," burst out of Casey, even though she knew she should stay quiet.

"What kind of a name is Calvin for a dog, any-way?" Faye demanded.

The beautiful lady's big dark eyes had stopped dancing. She was deciding something. "It's so I can say Calvin is waiting for me at home. Because, when you look like this? Sometimes, men want to insist." She shrugged, without looking at Faye, or Casey, or Calvin. It was as if she was already somewhere else. "Look, Calvin's used to being alone. So maybe your daughter—while I'm gone? It'll only be a couple of days— Maybe your daughter will feed—"

"All right," Faye said then.

Casey stared at her mother and hoped she'd heard correctly.

The beautiful lady had no doubt. "You will? Oh thank you. Really. You don't know."

"The money better be there," Faye warned her.

"It is," the woman said, over her shoulder because she had already passed the grocery bag and leash to Faye and was halfway out the door. "Trust me."

This was of course just what Faye never did, with anybody. But two hundred dollars was two hundred dollars.

"I hope you *are* old enough," Faye warned Casey. "Because as far as I'm concerned, that dog could starve to death on the streets." Her voice was loud enough for the beautiful lady to hear, if she had been listening. But by that time, the red Mini had rounded the corner and Casey was seated on the floor, looking Calvin in the eye, scratching him under his chin, while Faye reached into the grocery bag to locate an unsealed envelope and pull out the ten twenty-dollar bills.

THREE

Waking up with something warm and heavy resting on your stomach was nothing that had ever happened to Casey before. Also, having the first thing you see be a pair of round, dark brown eyes, excited to have you looking back. "Better get down," she warned Calvin.

At some time in the night he had left his towel bed on the floor to join Casey, which Faye had forbidden. Urged by a small shove, he did jump down, but then he rose onto his hind legs, front legs on top of the mattress, to watch her. He wanted to be as close to her as possible, Casey knew. "There better not be any messes made in the house," her mother had warned as they said good night, so Casey pulled on a pair of jeans and a T-shirt and practically ran to the kitchen. She took Calvin's leash from the counter, clipped it onto his collar, and they went out the door together.

He squatted down, right by the walk. When he finished, he led her back to the door.

Casey grinned. This dog knew his own mind, and she guessed it was now on breakfast. "You're in a hurry," she remarked, pouring his kibble into the heavy china bowl that had come in his grocery bag.

Calvin's tail wagged and wagged, with every bite. Casey had never seen food disappear so quickly. Maybe because dogs couldn't talk and just concentrated on filling their stomachs? Not that Faye and Casey had actual conversations over breakfast, or dinner either. In the morning, the day's activities were organized: "I should put the chicken into a 350-degree oven at five, right?" and "Move the sheets to the dryer when you get home from school." In the evening, the day's doings were reported: "We started the Revolutionary War today" and "That's the best lab report I ever wrote. I'm hoping for a C."

Faye and Casey might not have that much to talk about, but there was enough to keep them at the table for about five times longer than it took Calvin to eat his breakfast, lap up some water, and go back to the door. Was he asking to be taken out again?

Well, if he was asking, she was answering. Casey clipped on the leash and took him back outside. There, she found that she had understood him perfectly, since he turned in two circles, arched his back, and deposited his mess in the grass. After that, he trotted right back to the door. "Okay," she said, following him. "I get it. You're a good dog, Calvin, and smart, too."

His stubby tail wagged.

Faye held the door open for them. "You're not going to just leave the mess out there," she greeted Casey. "Go pick it up."

Casey stared at her mother.

"Weren't there plastic bags in with its supplies?"

"But—"

"When you have a dog, you pick up its messes," Faye announced. "It goes with the territory. Turn the bag inside out over your hand, like a glove, then reverse it around the stuff. Nobody expects you to touch it. And drop it in the garbage. In the can outside."

Casey did what she'd been told. When she went back into the kitchen, Faye had returned to her bowl of oatmeal topped with frozen berries, her attention on the shopping list for the week's groceries. Calvin wagged his tail, to thank her maybe, or maybe because he was glad to see her.

Saturday mornings, Faye went in at eight thirty to restock the market's shelves with whatever the first wave of weekend shoppers had taken off them. When that was done, she did her own shopping, and had the total deducted from her week's paycheck. Sometimes, although not often, a few dollars were left over. Those went into the Savings Envelope, until that held a hundred dollars, which was then taken to the bank. That was the way Faye saved, slow and steady.

Now that they had their own house, and especially with Calvin to look after, there was no question of Casey going along with her mother, to sit reading in a corner of the storeroom while Faye worked. Casey planned to take Calvin all the way around the block, a walk she hadn't yet taken herself. "It'll be nice for Calvin to see what else there is in the neighborhood," she said.

"Take plastic bags with you," Faye responded.

Faye liked to double-check things, to be certain. Casey got that about her mother.

Once she had swept all the rooms and scoured the bathroom, Casey clipped on the leash and they set off. Around the block wasn't much of a walk, she knew, but it felt to her like an adventure. Casey Hooper was walking a dog. Casey and Calvin were exploring the neighborhood together. She couldn't stop smiling.

She turned right onto Daisy Lane, not her usual left to the bus stop. From behind them, Lizzie barked a couple of times, standing at her fence, watching them walk away. Only one of the houses they passed going this way had a fenced yard, so Calvin could trot out to the end of his leash, going onto grass to squat and pee, and then trot right back to Casey. She bent to stroke his head, wondering what he would do if she let him off the leash. Would he run away? Would he come to her if she called him? Probably it would be smart to practice that inside the house first, someplace where he couldn't outrun her and disappear.

When Daisy Lane ended they turned right onto Marigold Street, which looked a lot like Daisy Lane, with its houses of various styles and sizes (none as small as theirs, but none particularly large or fancy either), each on its own lawn. Some had porches, or a garage, or flower gardens. Some had swings in the backyards, or bicycles lying up against front steps. Only a couple of cars drove along the street as she and Calvin made their way, looking (or sniffing) all around. Ahead of them, a woman in a pale blue jogging suit drew farther and farther ahead, and Spot ran at her side. Every now and then, Calvin looked back to be sure Casey was still there, at the other end of his leash, but mostly he explored, his nose on the sidewalk, in the grass, at a telephone pole. Once, she had to jerk him back, sharply, away from a flower bed. She didn't know if he would try to dig in it because she didn't know what he was like, but she didn't want to risk it.

A girl was Rollerblading on the opposite sidewalk, until she crossed the street to come to a halt right in front of them.

Casey pulled Calvin in close and safe.

"Is that a new dog?" the girl asked. "I haven't seen you with a dog before. Is it a rescue? It looks like a rescue." Someone, probably her mother, had French-braided her pale brown hair. Unless she had done it herself?

"I don't know," Casey admitted.

Calvin looked up at her, probably wondering why they had stopped.

"You don't know if it's a rescue?" the girl asked, staring out of blue eyes.

Casey was watching Calvin, who wagged his tail and nudged her calf with a cold nose. It was almost as good as if he said it in words: *Let's go!*

"I've seen you in school," the girl said.

Now Casey stared. "I didn't see you."

The girl laughed. "How could you when you're always looking at the floor. You look different this morning."

"Zoe?" a voice called from the house beside them,

where another girl with French braids held the door open. "Mom's already in the car!"

"Sorry," said the girl. "I'm Zoe, what's your name?"

"Casey Hoo—"

"Zoe! Come on!"

"We're going to the mall," the girl explained. "Evvie's a new friend so this is the first time I'm meeting her mother so . . ." She shrugged and Rollerbladed up the driveway.

"Come on, Calvin." Casey was not at all sorry to be the girl walking a dog rather than the girl going to the mall. Although she did wonder if Calvin was a rescue. Not that that mattered.

Oddly enough, that exact moment was when she remembered her wish.

She had wished for a dog.

She had wished for a dog and now she had one. Except not really. He was only temporary. So it was that kind of magic, the kind that would trick you if you let it. That didn't seem fair.

Magic wasn't fair, though, was it?

Unless it wasn't really magic, just coincidence.

Still, even with all the dreaming and wishing she'd done, Casey hadn't known just how wonderful it would be, having even just a temporary dog. That made it worse to remember she was going to have to give him back. She reminded herself that she had another whole day, plus this afternoon, with him. For the next day and a half, Casey Hooper had a dog. She already loved Calvin and she thought he loved her back. Or, at least, he liked her. They walked down Marigold Street, Calvin trotting along with his stub of a tail raised and Casey smiling.

A sudden jerk on the leash wiped the smile from her face. She tightened her grip while Calvin jerked hard, again, bolting forward. He was barking, too. She couldn't see anything wrong but he was pulling her up to a tree trunk. "You!" a voice yelled. "You, girl! Get your dog out of my yard! You hear?"

"No Calvin!" Casey pulled back on the leash. "Stop!"

She saw a cat perched on a branch overhead, hissing down at the dog who was trying to climb the tree after it.

Casey pulled back hard. She slid the switch to retract the line, and hold it. Close to her side now, Calvin strained against his collar but she was stronger than he was. His paws scrabbled on the ground, pulling against her.

"Get that dog off my cat!"

The angry voice belonged to a woman with a broom. She ran at Casey, sweeping at Calvin with the broom.

"That's the one!" she shouted over her shoulder to the short, round man standing on the porch steps behind her. "That's the one that keeps making his filthy messes on our lawn."

The man started down the steps, and Casey backed away. Calvin strained toward the tree. "He never!" she called. "I'm sorry about the cat," she called, and sort of meant it. It wasn't the cat's fault. "Come on, Calvin. Never mind them." She jerked on the leash and this time Calvin obeyed.

It felt strange, being yelled at, and yelling back, too, and at a grown-up. Her heart wouldn't slow down. Calvin had already forgotten about his thwarted chase, but Casey hadn't, and neither had the two angry people behind her. The man shouted after them, "And don't come back!"

Casey wasn't used to people being angry at her. Mostly, people didn't notice her, because she was good at being no trouble. Also, Faye didn't waste energy getting angry. She just announced things, like "You're not ever going to color in a book again," in a voice that told Casey she'd for sure lose all her crayons forever if she did.

But those two—probably a man and his wife and not very old, graying hair but young enough to charge across the yard waving a broom—they had been angry, and at her personally. Casey knew she had never set foot on Marigold Street before and she guessed that Calvin hadn't either, because she'd never seen the beautiful lady walking her dog. What made those two so angry? She didn't plan to find out. She'd never go near that yard again, that was for sure.

"You're a good dog, Calvin," she told him as they approached the corner of Bluebell Lane, where they turned right again. "They were just stupid mean people. You didn't do anything bad."

Everything's okay, she thought, even though the sight of another older couple walking toward them, on their same side of the street, made her nervous. She shortened Calvin's leash again and crossed the street, just in case. Because there were always things she didn't know. The woman, who looked a lot younger than her white-haired husband, stared at Casey for a minute but said nothing. Casey kept her eyes on the sidewalk ahead and pretended not to notice, but when they had turned right onto Bluebell Lane, the third side of the block, she still kept Calvin close to her side.

FOUR

Back on Daisy Lane, Calvin seemed to think he was going home. He stopped at his own gate and looked up at her.

"Not yet, Calvin," she told him.

His stubby tail wagged, as if to say, *You don't get it. This is my house where I live.*

She knew he couldn't understand words but she answered him anyway. "Not until late tomorrow," she explained. Then she had an idea. "Let's go!" she said, putting excitement into her voice. "Let's run!"

They ran together, side by side, all the rest of the way home.

When Faye returned, she carried two totes full of groceries. While they were washing the fruit and putting pasta boxes and canned tomatoes on shelves, milk and cheese and meat into the refrigerator, Calvin tried to stay close to Casey. He might have thought he was helping, or he might be feeling uneasy. After all, he'd had someone angry at him for no reason, and then he was still in this strange house with new people, one of whom he had to sense didn't want him there. Casey made a point of bending down to pet him whenever he got tangled up in her feet.

Faye wasn't sympathetic. "Can't you keep him out of the kitchen?"

So Casey called Calvin into her room and left him there, behind a closed door. He started whining right away, and they heard his nails scratch on the door.

"He'll ruin the wood," Faye said. "Get him out of there before he loses us the deposit."

After Casey let him out, Faye stood with her hands on her hips, staring down at him. "He'll stay out of my way if he knows what's good for him," she announced, so Casey took Calvin by his brown leather collar and walked him over to his water bowl by the door. She waggled her fingers in the water saying, "Come here, Calvin. Have some water. Then stay, stay here." She patted her palm on the floor, to help him know what to do.

His eyes looked sad to her, and confused. He couldn't know what had hit him, this poor dog who was not in his own familiar home, with his own familiar person. He couldn't understand that it would all be over soon. But he did seem to understand about Faye because he lay down on the floor right in front of the door and stayed there.

They finished putting away groceries and made grilled cheese sandwiches. Soon they carried dirty plates and glasses to the sink, and returned to the table, to read. Even when the long room filled with the silence of two people reading, Calvin didn't come to sit by Casey's legs.

After forty-five minutes, Faye closed her book and stood up. She looked at Casey, who usually went along with her mother to the pizzeria on Saturday afternoons. Saturday afternoon delivery was the slowest, most unpopular shift, but Paco had to have a delivery person regardless. Faye never earned many tips, but there was a hidden benefit. Sometimes, an order got filled and nobody picked it up, for reasons Paco liked to make up stories about: maybe they'd won the lottery and decided to have dinner in a fancy restaurant, or maybe they'd been kidnapped, or—most likely—maybe they discovered they couldn't afford their pizza after all and were too ashamed to call and say so. The possibilities were endless, but when that happened, for who-cared-what reason, Faye and Casey came home with a free pizza for their supper.

Casey enjoyed Saturday afternoons at the pizzeria. She liked sitting at a small table near the cash register, watching customers come and go, listening to their conversations or reading, and she liked going with her mother to various parts of the city to deliver pizzas. She liked the way Paco teased her, even if she never had anything smart to say back to him. And she really liked the way he teased Faye, pretending to be afraid of her, backing away dramatically, with his palms raised in horror, when she got impatient about something. Paco talked in over-elegant language to Faye, using his dark eyebrows to emphasize his words, and a lot of waving about of his hands. "If the signorina would be so kind as to bear these two pizzas to the address inscribed hereupon and return with all good speed, should we need her for another mission?" he asked, eyebrows up, hands gesturing.

Faye was never sure how to answer Paco. Usually she huffed and offered a sarcastic "I don't know who you're performing for," but sometimes Casey caught a small smile sneaking onto her mother's face. Casey guessed that Paco liked her mother. His dark eyes lingered on her and he was always wearing a clean shirt under an equally clean apron when they arrived. Also, there was the warmth with which he welcomed them, every Saturday, as if he'd been afraid they wouldn't come. Faye wasn't having any of this, of course. Faye was all prickles and keep-off signs. Hugging Faye would be like hugging a cactus. Not that Faye hugged anybody. That wasn't her way. Casey had thought about her mother, and figured she was Faye's chance to do things right, and her reason, too. Casey guessed that she was the reason Faye had made her plan, and made herself stick to it no matter how long it took. Casey never wished she didn't have Faye for a mother. She just wanted to have a dog, too.

That reminded her. "May I stay home today with Calvin? He'll need another walk this afternoon."

"I'd assumed you would," Faye answered. "Paco will be disappointed."

"What should I do about supper?" Casey wondered.

"There are always hot dogs," Faye said, heading out.

Faye would never say it out loud, but she had to be hoping for pizza, too.

FIVE

When it was just the two of them, Casey asked Calvin to be patient, just for a minute, because she had an idea. He wagged his tail and looked up at her, as if to say, *Sure, okay, no problem, I trust you.*

Casey liked the way that look made her feel. In fact, she felt pleased with herself. Casey Hooper had a dog and a good idea! Maybe a good idea, she reminded herself, opening the drawer where they kept worn-out clothes, socks, and dish towels, and tees, anything you could use as a rag.

It really was a good idea, too, once Calvin learned that he was supposed to chase after the thick cloth ball Casey made, and bring it back to her so she could throw it again.

After playing for quite a while, including the delay when the ball came unknotted so that she and Calvin engaged in a long and enjoyable tug-of-war with it, she decided it was time for a walk. They set off down Daisy Lane.

This time, she turned left. Lizzie wasn't in sight so they didn't have to feel bad about leaving her behind when they turned right onto Garden Street. They walked together, although Calvin sometimes went to examine something. Casey couldn't know what he was thinking as he sniffed and squatted, and made one mess which she immediately bagged up, and trotted ahead with his ears cocked or came back to check on her. She could only know how she felt, walking her dog. She felt special, for some reason, and comfortable, too, as if she belonged here, on this street, with her dog.

There were no dogs behind fences on Garden Street, but as soon as they turned right onto Aster Lane there were several fenced yards, and several dogs inhabiting them. A couple of times, Casey and Calvin were barked at, but no more than a couple of quick warning barks to say, *I see you, better stay on the sidewalk!* At the end of the block, they turned right again onto Marigold, where a familiar figure walked toward her. She recognized the small shape and white hair of the old man from that morning. His wife wasn't with him but he came up to Casey as if she was the very person he was looking for.

Maybe he knew Calvin. Calvin was wagging his tail.

"It's time for lunch," he told Casey. He looked right into her face. His eyes were pale brown, his eyebrows almost invisible, and he wasn't very tall.

"Is it?" she asked. Well, different people ate their meals at different times.

"I'm Arthur," he said. "Pleased to meet you."

She hadn't planned to introduce herself but it was the polite thing to do and Faye emphasized politeness, so, "I'm Casey. This is Calvin," Casey said.

He ignored Calvin. "Do you live around here?" he asked, waving a hand in front of him.

"On Daisy Lane."

"I don't live on Daisy Lane," he said, and nodded his head wisely, as if that was an important thing for her to know.

This conversation confused Casey and, from the look on his face, it confused Arthur, too. Maybe that was why Casey didn't feel as tongue-tied as usual. Or maybe it was his buttoned-wrong sweater, which hung down lower on one side than the other. She felt a little sorry for him. Although, maybe old people always looked like this. There were no old people in Casey's life, not even grandparents, so she couldn't be sure.

"I don't live in your house," Arthur explained. "We

should get going. There's lunch, and dogs need water to drink."

Casey didn't really know how to respond, but he didn't seem like anyone she needed to be afraid of. Also, she had Calvin to protect her, if she needed protection. "Which house is yours?" she asked.

But he didn't seem to hear her. Instead, he held gently to her arm and they continued on together along Marigold Street.

"Dad! Dad?" a woman called from behind them. "Where are you—? Little girl? Wait up, little girl! Please!"

Casey stopped. Arthur stopped. Calvin stopped. He sat on the sidewalk, wagged his tail, and watched Casey.

The woman from that morning jogged toward them. She slowed to a walk when she saw that they had stopped. "It's your wife," Casey told Arthur.

"You know perfectly well that Mary's dead," he answered sharply.

"Oh. She's your daughter."

"Well I know that," he answered, and laughed. "Don't you think I know my own girl? Louise," he greeted the woman. "What's gotten into you? You're in no shape to go running around like that."

"Dad," she answered, and took his arm, taking control and responsibility. "I didn't hear him leave the house," she told Casey. "I'm sorry. Are you all right? You don't ever need to be frightened of Dad, you know, he's just . . ." Her voice tapered off. She patted her father's arm and kissed his cheek. "He's a pussy-cat, aren't you, Dad."

"It's what your mother always says." He smiled.

Arthur's daughter Louise had a round, friendly face, with lots of worry lines. She had her father's brown eyes, only not so faded.

"I'm fine," Casey said.

"Of course she's all right, except her dog is thirsty and— Loulou? Let me introduce my friend Kate and her dog— I don't know your dog's name," he said to Casey.

"Calvin," she told him. "It's Casey, not Kate," she told his daughter.

Arthur ignored her. "We were having a nice talk, me and Kate," he complained.

The daughter grimaced, and shrugged, and said, "Sorry, Dad." She didn't seem to know what to say to Casey. Then, "I don't think I've seen you before?"

"We're new. I live around the corner, on Daisy Lane."

"Lucky for us you do. I am sorry. Usually he's—"

"Don't worry. It's okay."

Casey had figured it out.

"I'll take him home," Louise said.

"You can come too, Cathy," said Arthur.

Louise gave a quick shake of her head, so Casey said, "I can't just now. Calvin is thirsty."

Arthur nodded wisely. "Dogs need a lot of water. Come see us later, won't you?"

Casey looked at Louise and then back to Arthur. "Okay," she said, certain that the woman knew it wasn't going to happen and pretty sure that the man would have forgotten about it by the time his daughter had him safely back in their own house.

"Thank you, Casey," Louise said.

"You know her name?" Arthur was asking as Casey led Calvin away.

When they arrived back on Daisy Lane, Lizzie was just coming out of her yard, with a man. Calvin pulled at his leash, trying to get to Lizzie, who was pulling at the end of her own leash, trying to get to Calvin. The two dogs met in front of Casey's house. The man grinned at Casey. "They're friends."

"I know," Casey said.

The two dogs were sniffing and circling one another, the way dog friends do.

"My wife told me about you," the man said. He was young and smiled easily. "You're the girl who likes dogs."

Casey didn't deny it.

"There can't be much wrong with someone who likes dogs." The man laughed. "C'mon, Lizzie, there's miles to go before we sleep."

Casey watched them walk off down the street, the tall, long-legged, dark-haired man in jeans and the short-legged, chunky dog trotting to keep up with him. Calvin jerked on his leash; he wanted to go with them. But Casey didn't and she was the one in charge.

When Faye came home with a pizza and it was sausage and mushrooms, it became the most perfect day Casey had ever lived. She had walked her dog and played with her dog, all day long, and now they were having pizza for supper which meant she could give Calvin what Paco called pizza bones. Casey took the narrow leftover crust she'd saved from her first slice and offered it to Calvin.

"Don't do that," Faye said, sharp and quick.

Casey jerked her hand, and the crust, back. Calvin

was already on his feet when Faye spoke but he lay right down.

"No animals get fed at my table," said Faye, not looking at Calvin. "Even if they come begging." She paused for a bit, then added, "Especially if they come begging."

"But he wasn't," Casey argued.

Faye just looked at her.

"Really! It was all my idea. He didn't have anything to do with it."

Then Faye did look at the dog, but only to say, "Get away. Away from the table. You heard me, go! Scat!"

Maybe he did understand words, because Calvin went to lie down by the door, resting his head on his front paws. He looked from Faye to Casey and back to Faye, his eyes sad.

Faye didn't care. When it came to the dog, she was all cactus. Casey knew her mother was in it only for the money, and she understood how important the money was to both of them. But she couldn't help wishing . . .

That old, familiar, longing feeling reminded Casey that she still had a second wish. But if Calvin belonged to the beautiful lady, and Faye was Casey's mother, and only relative, too, how could a wish help? If she wished that Faye would change her mind, or, really, change what was in her heart, or not in her heart, so she'd begin to like Calvin, the dog still belonged to somebody else. If she wished Calvin was hers to keep, what would have to happen to make that possible? Something to Faye, most likely, and without Faye, how could Casey survive? Or did Casey want the beautiful lady to die so she could have a dog? Even then, Faye wouldn't go along with it; Casey knew that.

What wish was possible, under these circumstances? When the first wish had already tricked her.

Casey and Faye worked and read at their desks all that evening. They sat with their backs to one another and the only sounds in the house were studying noises like the rustle of paper or the faint ticking of a keyboard. Calvin lay by the door watching them. He was hoping to be called over, Casey knew. He wanted to be close and petted, but he seemed to know better than to try that around Faye. Casey went to her room, and to bed, early. Calvin came with her. Faye paid no attention to what the dog did, as if he didn't exist.

SIX

Sunday mornings, Faye took an hour for herself—for her hair, for a long soak in the tub, to trim and shape her nails. Casey's Sunday job was to wash and dry their sheets and towels. "Clean, conditioned hair? Clean sheets and towels? I can make it through another week," Faye liked to say, setting off in black trousers and a white shirt for her weekly student aid job, serving at the Faculty Club Sunday brunch buffet. There were no tips but as student-aid jobs went, this was a good one. That Sunday, instead of being settled with a book at the university library to wait for her mother to join her for a picnic sandwich, consumed in the few minutes between brunch service and her afternoon study group, Casey got to stay home with Calvin.

Although staying home wasn't what they did, Casey and Calvin. After making the beds and hanging up the clean towels, they took a long, figure-eight walk, right onto Daisy Lane then right onto Marigold Street, right onto Bluebell Lane and right onto Garden, right back up Daisy but then left onto Marigold and left onto Aster, left on Garden, left onto Daisy and then, all the way around the figure eight again. They kept as far away as they could from the house where the cat couple lived but otherwise they followed their noses, especially Calvin's nose.

They ran into Arthur and Louise on their second trip along Marigold. "This is my new friend, Cathy, and her dog," Arthur announced to Louise, as if he had forgotten that they had all met the afternoon before. "We were at the park," he told Casey. "You should take your dog there. Dogs like parks, I remember. It's not far. Is it far, Loulou?"

"Three blocks. Do you know it, Casey? There's a dog park, too. Your dog might like it," Louise said.

"Calvin's not mine," Casey admitted.

"Oh. Well, you look like you belong together. So you're just walking her?" Louse asked.

"Him," Casey corrected, but with a smile. There was something about these two that made her glad to see them. "He's boarding with us, just for the weekend," she explained, careful not to sound too sad.

"Oh," Louise said again. "Well, we have to be going."

"But we just got here," Arthur objected.

"It's time, Dad," she said. "We have lunch to get ready."

Arthur winked at Casey. "We all know how much Loulou likes her lunch."

Louise laughed softly, and took his arm. They walked away.

Casey and Calvin had a picnic lunch in their backyard, consisting of a peanut-butter-and-jelly sandwich for Casey, with a glass of milk, and two saved pizza bones for Calvin. They played chase and fetch with the cloth ball for a while, then went inside to do homework (Casey) and nap (Calvin). By midafternoon, they were ready for another walk.

Casey had decided to repeat the figure eight but they were stopped right away by Lizzie, who was leaving her yard with the man. Calvin and Lizzie greeted one another with wagging tails and the usual dog sniffings. Calvin even gave a couple of little growls, pretending something. They made Casey feel like laughing, those dogs. Lizzie's man seemed to feel the same. Like Casey, he waited patiently at his end of the leash, watching.

After a minute he said, "We're going to the dog park. You could—"

Her head was shaking no.

"Calvin loves it there. She's a sociable little thing but she doesn't get much chance to play with other dogs, with Lina's work schedule."

"He," Casey mumbled, flushing.

The man looked worried. "Actually? She." As if he knew Calvin better than Casey did.

Casey didn't argue. She stared silently down at the top of Calvin's head.

"Okay," he said. "But is there something about me? Are you— You're not afraid of me, are you?"

"No," she mumbled, because she wasn't. Not afraid. It was just—other people, especially kids?—they made her uneasy.

"You could go to the park on your own. Because Calvin likes it so much, as I happen to know, since usually Lina leaves her with us when she's away."

"Him," Casey contradicted again.

"Hunh," the man said. "If— What *is* your name? I know you just moved in, my wife has told me about you. I'm Eddy, by the way. You've met Lizzie, and my wife, Alba's her name, you've waved at her, haven't you?"

"I'm Casey," she said, because it would be so rude not to.

"Okay, Casey, then tell me: Does Calvin squat to pee? Or raise a leg against a tree trunk, or a signpost?"

Casey's glance snapped up to his face. "He squats."

"Females squat. Males raise a leg."

Casey felt herself flushing again.

"Live and learn," Eddy said, with a big smile, lots of teeth. "Not knowing something's nothing to be embarrassed about, Casey."

She couldn't help smiling back. "I guess."

"When's Lina getting back?"

Lina, Casey had deduced, was the beautiful lady. "Tonight, she said."

"I should warn you, Lina puts her career first."

Casey's heart lifted. "She might be later than she said?"

"Sometimes she is, although often she isn't. She's ambitious, and she should be, she's really good. Anyway, Lizzie and I really do have to get going. It used to be the three of us taking walks together but—Alba's having a baby, see, and her doctor says she has to stay in bed for these last four weeks. So it's only me and Lizzie. Isn't it, girl?" he asked his dog, who looked up at him eagerly. "Are you sure you and Calvin don't want to come along?"

Half of Casey did, and probably all of Calvin, but Faye would be home by five so she shook her head.

"Okay," he said, but he had another question. "It's just you and your mom?"

Casey nodded.

"She's not home very much."

"She's going to school and she has jobs."

"I guess she's a hard worker," he observed. "Can I ask, what about your dad?"

Casey stared right at his face. She shook her head. No.

"Oh," he mumbled, and now he was the one with flushed cheeks looking down at his dog. "Sorry, I shouldn't— Anyway." He looked up, smiling, but his dark eyes were sad for her. "Maybe another day at the dog park?" He walked away, pity trailing behind him like a snail's slime track.

That walk was over before it began. Once Casey was safely back in her house, she unclipped Calvin's leash, refilled his water bowl, and left him there, happily lapping.

She continued on into her bedroom. There was no

need to close the door; she had the house to herself. She stood beside her bed, staring down at the pillow but not seeing it. She lined her thoughts up, a row of soldiers. She'd thought about this father question. Of course she had and especially when she was little, because people seemed to think little children understood only half of what was said around them. So Casey had considered the question and she'd decided that if you never had a father, you can't mind his absence the way you can if, for example, your married parents decide to get a divorce.

How could you, when all you were doing without was something you'd never had? Casey knew what steak was, but she'd never missed it, had she? Faye said that when Casey got older, maybe thirteen or so, she might mind it more about not having a father, but Faye didn't know everything.

And if Faye turned out to be right?

Casey would deal with that if and when it happened. It had never been a father she'd wished for. It was a dog. It had always been a dog.

Calvin's head butted up against her calf, reminding Casey that he—she—was there, right then, beside her.

Except, Casey hadn't wished wisely enough.

But she had one wish left, didn't she?

Except, Faye simply didn't like Calvin. And it wasn't only Calvin, it was any dog. So Casey needed two more wishes, one for Faye and one for a dog. . . .

The pillow stared back at her, flat and white and hopeless: because now that she had Calvin, it wasn't any dog she wished for. It was Calvin. Only Calvin.

Okay, Casey Hooper said to herself. *It is what it is and too bad.* "I'm sorry, Calvin," she said, crouching down to look her dog in the eye. Calvin was sorry, too, Casey was sure of it.

When someone knocked on their door just as they finished supper, Casey looked at her mother, who grumbled, "She's not exactly early," and went on eating while Casey got up to answer it. She also expected it would be the beautiful woman, Lina, on the other side of the screen, but it was Eddy instead.

"Is your mother—" is all he had time to say before Faye joined her daughter to announce, "We're not buying anything."

Eddy smiled his easy, friendly smile and said, "I'm not selling. I'm hoping to hire Casey—"

"How do you know my daughter?" Faye demanded, all cactus. She held the handle to be sure the screen door stayed closed. "Go finish your supper," she told

Casey, even though she knew Casey's plate was clean. "And take it with you." Meaning Calvin.

Casey knew better than to argue. She sat at the table, her back to the door, and listened.

"I met her because of the dogs. Just this afternoon. My wife and I live just down the street, our dog Lizzie and Calvin are friendly. We're your neighbors," Eddy said.

"And?" Faye asked.

"I'd like to hire Casey to walk our dog."

"I don't think so," Faye said.

"If you'd reconsider?" Eddy asked, clearly surprised. He tried again. "The thing is, my wife's pregnant. She's been put on bed rest, doctor's orders, and I'm gone all day. It would be a big help to us," he said, more loudly now because Faye was walking away. "If you change your mind—?"

Faye didn't bother telling him she wasn't in the business of changing her mind.

Nobody else, especially not the beautiful lady, Lina, had come to the door when Faye told Casey it was time for them to go to bed. "I hope she doesn't think I'm waiting up for her," Faye said as they packed their books for the next day. "She can just wait until morning to get her dog back," Faye announced, and turned out the lights.

SEVEN

Casey went to bed sad and Monday morning she woke up sad. Her spirits soggy with sadness, she walked Calvin down to her real home and opened the gate so both of them could go in. She set the dog's supplies on the step by Lina's front door. After she latched the gate behind herself, she turned back to promise Calvin, "She's coming home today."

Calvin wagged her tail and reached her nose through the pickets to lick Casey's hand, as if she understood. At least, Casey thought, Calvin didn't have to be sad. Calvin was getting her old life back. So was Casey, except hers wasn't exactly the life she wanted.

Casey made it a normal coming-home-from-school Monday afternoon. She stopped to greet Fritz and then Henri, then Spot. She spent time with Calvin, then Lizzie, like always. That Monday, however, there was a difference. Only a small one, but Eddy's wife,

Alba, called down to her, "Hey, Casey. Hello. Have a good day at school?"

How did you answer that? When someone who didn't know you was asking. A little surprised at the question, Casey called back, "I guess," and then she wondered, *Was it a good day*? She had been smiled at across the lunchroom by Zoe and all of last week's homework had been returned to her, with only a few red marks, even math: it had been an okay school day, better than before, but was that actually good? Without Calvin, could any day be good?

In her house, things were back to completely normal, empty and silent. When Faye returned from waiting tables at the restaurant, she found Casey alone, doing math problems at her desk. "Good," was Faye's only comment, before she removed her own books from the carrier bag she used for school.

Over a supper of turkey meatloaf and rice, noticing Casey's mood, Faye advised, "Everything comes to an end. Good or bad, it ends. You can count on that." Casey knew that. She didn't argue when Faye announced, "You'll feel better in the morning."

Faye was probably right about that, too. And everything would have gone as Faye expected if, when Casey looked down the quiet street before going to her room that evening, she hadn't noticed that all the windows in Lina's house were dark. Seeing that, she opened the door and stepped outside to see more clearly, and couldn't see a red Mini parked in the driveway, glistening under the streetlight.

But the car was supposed to be there. On weeknights, the car was always there.

Casey walked out to the sidewalk, and then down Daisy Lane. Lizzie and all the other dogs were inside, so there was no barking. Calvin ran up to her fence to meet Casey and Casey saw that the grocery bag was just where she had left it, right beside the door. Was there anything else to do but take the dog, and the bag, back home with her? Even Faye, however unwillingly, had to agree.

"I'll put a note on the door," was all Faye said. "Letting her know where her dog is. I don't want to be woken up in the middle of the night."

It was the same on Tuesday, the same sad morning parting, the same resigned return from school. At eight o'clock, when no lights and no red Mini could be seen, Faye didn't insist that Casey wait until full dark before fetching Calvin. When they had returned, and Calvin had greeted Faye, who ignored her, all Faye asked was, "Is my note still on the door?"

Casey could report that Yes, it was.

By Wednesday, Casey parted from Calvin with an equal mix of sadness and hope. What was going on? Where was Lina? By Wednesday afternoon she allowed herself to smile when, after saying hello to Fritz and Henri and Spot, she saw that Faye's note was still stuck on Lina's front door when she stopped by to greet Calvin. When she had said hello to Lizzie and Alba called out her question about her day at school, Casey answered with a question of her own. "Where is Lina?"

"With Lina, you never know," said Alba.

"But what about Calvin?" Casey called.

"I know," Alba answered.

There was more hope than sadness in Casey, when she let herself into their house that Wednesday afternoon.

But that evening, when she went to bring Calvin and the grocery bag of supplies home again, Faye's note was gone. "That's a relief," Faye admitted. "I was beginning to think we were stuck with getting rid of it."

"There's still nobody in the house," Casey said. "You don't want to have to wait up until Lina gets home, so, what if Calvin sleeps here again? I'll take her back in the morning."

"I guess she knows where her dog is," Faye remarked. "If that woman's got any sense of fair play, she'll give us another two hundred."

Casey and Calvin retreated to Casey's bedroom.

Thursday afternoon, Alba had a lot to say, calling down from her window. "You might as well take Calvin with you now, Casey. What time does your mother get home? That is your mother, isn't she?"

"Yes. Why?"

"She just looks really young. To have such a big kid because—are you ten?"

"Eleven." Casey wasn't going to tell Alba more than that. Let her think Faye looked a lot younger than she actually was; their story was nobody else's business.

"Or did you mean why take Calvin now?" Alba asked.

Casey nodded, and maybe it was the truth.

"Eddy will explain to your mother. He gets home around half past five. What time do you eat?"

"Six," Casey said. "She gets home around five on Thursdays, but—"

"I'll text him," Alba called down, and she moved away from the window.

At five-thirty, Faye was prepared. She waited, one hand on the screen door handle, to be sure Eddy couldn't expect to come in. Casey sat at the table with Calvin at her feet, listening.

"Lina's not coming back," Eddy reported. "She's breaking her lease, and the landlord's already rented the house so he doesn't want the dog making messes in the yard."

"I can sympathize with that," Faye said.

Casey dropped a reassuring hand onto Calvin's head. Calvin twisted around to lick it.

"She called last night. Late. She wants us to take Calvin."

Calvin would like living with Lizzie, Casey told herself. It wasn't as if Calvin had lived with Casey very long. How could a dog be loyal after such a short time?

Nothing personal, she told herself.

"The trouble is—we're expecting. A baby . . ." He hesitated, as if waiting for Faye to say something. Since Faye didn't do what most people expected, after a minute it was Eddy who spoke again. "It hasn't been an easy pregnancy. They're going to do a C-section as soon as she's safely past the thirty-fourth week, which is still almost four weeks off."

Another hesitation. Another silence from Faye.

"So we just can't take Calvin, much as we'd like to. And after, there'll be the baby, and actually we were sort of hoping your daughter would be available to help out. With the baby, and our dog, Lizzie, she's a corgi. But about Calvin—"

"My daughter has school," Faye announced.

"It's almost summer," he argued. "Unless she has summer school?"

"Not my daughter."

"So she'll be— But I get it, she's your daughter, so I guess you decide, but—"

"That's right," Faye interrupted.

"But what about Calvin," he began, unhappily.

Faye said nothing.

"She's a rescue, but that was a couple of years ago when she was—"

"A puppy. Cute." Faye practically spat out the words.

Eddy was silent for a bit, then, "I'm sorry," he said. "For Calvin. And Casey, too. It's hard."

"What else is new," Faye said. It was not a question.

After Eddy left, Faye came to stand beside Casey and Calvin. Neither of them looked up at her.

"You know what I have to do," Faye said.

The top of Calvin's head wasn't very large, Casey thought. No bigger than her palm, really. Calvin's fur was poodle-ly curls, but soft, as milky a brown as Faye's morning coffee. Casey couldn't tell what Calvin might be looking at without bending down and she didn't dare move.

"I'll take her to the shelter Saturday, on my way to Paco's. You don't have to come with me, Casey. You can if you want to but you don't have to. The dog won't know the difference."

She would, Casey argued silently as she nodded her head without looking at her mother.

"I *am* sorry," Faye said, and it sounded like she meant it. For all the good her being sorry did Casey. Or Calvin. "I do wish things were different, but they aren't."

Then Casey did look up, because her mother sounded tired.

But Faye never got tired. Faye didn't give way and she didn't give up and she didn't get tired.

EIGHT

If Saturday had been the best day of Casey's life, that Friday was the worst. Saturday had been bright with sunshine and Friday was gray with rain, inside Casey as well as outside on the street. She almost played hooky, something she'd never wanted to do and never even thought of doing, however not particularly happy she might have been, in a classroom, in a school. But she left Calvin in her bedroom, just in case the dog made a mess, and splashed to the bus stop, trying to think of a way.

Through every class, Casey thought. Nobody seemed to notice her lack of attention. All day long she kept thinking, even if she knew there was no way to find. It was as if she'd been living in the Desert View Motel, with the shades pulled so far down all she could see was gas stations and strip malls. Then Calvin got into the room with her and it was all different, even if it was the same room. The door opened. The shades went up. Maybe the gas stations and strip malls were still there, but now Casey could see the wide sky too, stretched out blue over everything, with clouds floating in it and sometimes planes, flying off across distant hills. The room hadn't really changed but when Calvin was there, it felt different. Now the shades were back down and that open door was about to slam shut, and Casey couldn't do anything about it.

Even if someone had lifted the shades for her, Casey wasn't sure she had the heart to look out. Because if magic had already given her Calvin once, she still had one wish left but. . . . But how could Casey wish to keep Calvin without that same wish losing her her mother?

Casey understood how much she needed, and cared about, her strong, strict, demanding cactus of a mother. Still, giving up Calvin was making Casey sadder than she'd ever been before.

It had stopped raining, but Casey didn't have the heart to greet any dogs as she walked up Daisy Lane. Head down, seeing only the sidewalk under her feet, hearing only the soft pat-pat of sneakers on wet cement, she came home, and unlocked the door, and went in. First thing, she let Calvin out of the bedroom.

Calvin jumped up against Casey's thighs, making

odd moany whiny noises, as if trying to say something, then she rushed to the door.

Of course, she needed to go out. She'd been locked in all day. Casey didn't think to put on the leash. She remembered it only when Calvin raced out onto the grass and squatted. Then, of course, it was too late. If she went back inside to get the leash, Calvin could slip away, and get lost.

Would that be worse than going back to the shelter? A voice in Casey's head asked. She didn't even know if it was a no-kill shelter.

"Good girl," Casey said, using her voice to connect her to the dog. "You've had a long day. So have I. But we should—Calvin? Come," she said, as Calvin raised herself up, and shook herself vigorously, as if she was shaking off the long solitary hours.

"Come," Casey said again, and Calvin trotted right up to her. "Let's go inside and get your leash so we can take a nice walk," Casey said. Maybe later Calvin could run away, or maybe tomorrow morning?

That afternoon, they walked around one block and then around the other. There was a breeze now, not brisk enough to blow the clouds away but sometimes there was a moment of sunshine before there were clouds again, coming between Casey and the sun.

Casey and Calvin and the sun, that is. Casey and Calvin were together.

Inside of Casey, there was no sunshine. It was all gray and cold, and a damp sadness. Calvin seemed unaware of this. Her stubby tail was up and her nose down as she trotted eagerly from one smell to the next.

Arthur was sitting in a big chair on his front porch. He called to her, "Little girl?" but Casey just waved and walked on.

They walked the figure eight a second time because Casey didn't want to go back to her house. Not yet. Once she went inside, she would be waiting for Faye to get home from the restaurant and once Faye had come home, she would be waiting for dinner to be over, the day to end, and it to be Saturday.

When Faye would take Calvin to the shelter.

Lina should never have rescued Calvin if she was going to abandon her. If Lina had never rescued her, Casey would never have met her, and had her for almost a week, and had to have this sick sad feeling in her stomach.

On their second figure eight, Casey called to Arthur, "Hello Arthur!" and waved.

That time he remembered her name. "It's Casey," he called, waving, "and . . . with . . . Casey's dog."

When he said that, the sick feeling in Casey's stomach swelled up and then contracted, like an elastic band. She ran home and didn't even unclip the leash, just dropped it on the floor as she ran into her room, Calvin close at her heels dragging the leash which bounced off the floor, bump-bump-bump.

Casey stood in front of her bureau. Her head fell, until her forehead rested on its wooden top. Her shoulders hunched, trying to get closer to one another, as if that could protect her heart. She recognized the feeling, from years and years ago: she wanted to cry. It felt like needing to vomit but it wasn't exactly the same. It was a balloon of feeling swelling bigger and bigger inside of her until her heart had to—

And then she knew what she could wish. How she could say it.

All of the squeezing choking feelings disappeared.

Calvin stood pressed close up to Casey's leg. Before anything else, Casey bent down to unclip the leash and pet the dog gently, all the length of her short body. "It's all right," she told Calvin. "You're a good dog."

Calvin at her heels, Casey went out to her desk. She opened the center drawer and took out the gray tissue paper. She was slow and careful, thinking hard, trying to be wise.

Casey put the tissue down on the kitchen table and poured herself a glass of milk, thinking, choosing the words, making it the right wish. Because it wasn't a dog she needed to wish for now. It was Faye she needed to wish about. She thought of the words, the exact words, and finished her milk. She reviewed the wish she had decided on, like the final check before a spelling test: I wish Faye would open her heart to Calvin. Not a big change, just an important one. The only necessary one.

Carefully, she raised the tissue to her lips. Calvin was watching her, and she looked right into the dog's hopeful eyes. "I wish," she whispered, "that my mother—Faye Hooper," she added, in case there was some other Faye somewhere else in the world this wish (if it was a real magic wish) could fall on—"would open—"

There was a sound from somewhere, but she ignored it.

"—her heart—"

Someone grabbed her hand and pulled it from her mouth. The tissue melted away.

"Casey!" Faye shouted.

Casey's mother was pale and big eyed, all spines, and she had ruined the wish.

"Don't! Stop!" Faye cried. She sounded crazy, but they'd talked about drugs so Casey knew why.

"I'm not!" Casey yelled. "You don't understand!"

"Where is it? I want to see and you'll tell me who you got it from, my girl— Get that dog out from underfoot!"

That was more than Casey could stand. Faye was furious and Calvin was lost and Casey had used her last wish.

"I trusted you!" Faye cried. "Casey! You have to show me!"

Casey was sobbing. She sank down onto the floor and gathered Calvin onto her lap and sobbed into the dog's soft coat. Calvin twisted around to lick at her face, which only made her cry harder.

Faye was searching for whatever it was her daughter had been about to swallow or smoke and not finding anything. She was taking deep breaths and blowing them slowly out.

"Okay," Faye said, eventually. "It's okay. I'm sorry, Casey. Just tell me. What was it? Casey? Please, say something. I mean, should I call 911?"

Faye wasn't yelling now and Casey knew she hadn't really been angry. Faye was frightened, because she didn't want anything bad to happen to her daughter.

Casey knew that. She understood. "No," she gulped out, between sobs. "Don't. It's not—I promise—"

"Okay," Faye said, "Okay. Let's calm down." She sat down beside Casey on the floor, close enough so their shoulders were touching.

Casey ignored her mother. She kept her arms around Calvin and let her tears drip—quietly now, at least she'd stopped sobbing—into the dog's soft curls. She couldn't stop feeling bad, for the lost wish, and the dog she was about to lose, with their one chance to stay together now gone forever.

Before she stood up again, Faye rested a hand on Casey's head.

Casey stayed where she was. She heard her mother move her bag to her desk, use the bathroom, run water for a cool drink. Every time, Faye's steps came close to Casey and hesitated there before going on. But Casey couldn't stop crying. She couldn't look up.

Even when somebody knocked on the door she didn't look up. Even when Faye asked, "What do you want?" and then "Who are you?" and "How do you know Casey?" she kept her face buried.

It was a woman. Her voice wasn't familiar, but it wasn't unfamiliar either. "May I come in?" she asked. "Please? I can't be away very long."

She sounded anxious, and she was upset, too.

But Faye never let anyone past their front door.

"It's my father. I'm responsible for him. There's nobody else, but I—"

Faye didn't say anything and Casey knew that if she looked she would see a huge, needle-y cactus planted in the doorway, to keep people out.

"—sometimes I need just an hour off, just every now and then or—"

Another silence.

"Or he'll have to go away. I'll have to put him into care. He won't understand and I'll feel terrible, forever. My husband couldn't— He left but if Casey and her dog could just come and sit with him while I—go to the store, or the library—because I love him, and because he was always there for me. But— "

"Come in," Faye was saying, and that did raise Casey's face from its safe hiding place. "Come in, let me— Can I make you a cup of tea?"

Casey stared at her mother's back.

"Thank you, no, I have to get back, he's alone, but if Casey—"

"What's wrong with him?" Faye asked.

"He gets confused, that's all. He's old and—I can pay her, not much but—"

"We can always use a little money," Faye allowed.

"Dad has taken a shine to her, her and her little dog."

"Calvin," Faye said. "Yes. They're quite a pair, those two."

But it sounded as if Faye could be smiling.

From the back Faye didn't look different. Except, "We didn't plan on having a dog," Faye was saying as she turned her head to look back at Casey and Calvin. "But I guess we do."

And yes, there was a smile, sneaking in.

THE UNICORN

ONE

As soon as he saw that word, Billy knew what he'd wish for. He took one of the tissues and said to it, in a magic-worthy whisper, "I wish I had a real, live unicorn."

The tissue disappeared from between his fingers and so did the note with its cautionary message and the envelope the note came in that had only his name, BILLY FAIRFIELD, on the front. This left just one thin gray piece of tissue paper, which he put into the drawer with his socks. In this climate, Billy could always wear slides unless it was some fancy dress-up dinner which almost never happened; he could be sure that nobody would be putting clean socks into that drawer. The wish-tissue would be safe.

He'd be the only person in the whole world who had a real, live unicorn. He might be only ten years old but he'd read the stories and he'd googled it, too, and he knew. In the stories it was girls—maidens they called them back then—who tamed unicorns, but why shouldn't a boy do it? Girls weren't smarter or stronger or more important than boys; everybody who knew anything knew they were equal. In this world, everybody was pretty much the same. People had finally figured that out.

Billy fell asleep wondering how he'd get his unicorn. Maybe Amazon? Could it arrive in a UPS truck, or FedEx? He wouldn't find it in any store, even the fanciest, for the obvious reason. So maybe his unicorn would just trot up to the gates and touch the keypad with its horn and the gates would swing open: magic. Or his unicorn could arrive in the night and be standing at the foot of Billy's bed when he woke up.

That wasn't how it happened.

TWO

How it happened was:

Billy awoke to no unicorn at the foot of his bed, and none waiting at the bottom of the stairs when he went down to the breakfast room. Equally, no unicorn stood at the table or emerged from the kitchen with his pancakes, bacon, orange juice, and milk. No unicorn greeted him in his bathroom, either, or waited with his backpack at the door, or stood watching beside the car when he got into the back seat to be driven to school.

But didn't he glimpse something white? A flash of shining white among the woods that shielded his home from anybody trying to look in? That had to be his unicorn.

The day dragged by, class after class, recess after recess, snack, lunch, and even sports took a long time to come to an end. By the time he got home again, Billy was so impatient to get his unicorn that he just dropped his backpack in the foyer and went right back outside.

But the unicorn wasn't waiting there for him.

So it had to be hiding in the woods, near the gates, where he'd seen the flash of white that morning. Was it hiding from him? It couldn't be, and he was going to go down the drive to find it. The drive was over a mile long, which would take a long time to walk. Luckily, Billy had a Onewheel. He stepped on the board and set it off as fast as it could go back down the winding driveway, steering around the curves while looking everywhere, ahead, around, back over his shoulder so as not to miss his unicorn. The Onewheel could move over grass just as easily as on the paved drive, so once they met up, he and his unicorn could go wherever they wanted, to hang out.

When he couldn't see his unicorn among the beeches and maples and evergreens, Billy decided that the next best place to look was the gardens. He searched the flower garden first, since flowers and unicorns seemed like a good match, and then in the vegetable garden, because unicorns were herbivores, weren't they? Next he tried the herb garden, because it was old-fashioned and unicorns were old-fashioned things, and finally he looked in the untidy English garden, where things grew a little wilder. Unicorns came from the time of King Arthur and his knights, and they were mostly English, Billy knew.

But his unicorn was nowhere to be seen. It couldn't be hiding from him, could it? Although, probably like other animals, it needed to find a watering hole. Billy guided his Onewheel through a little wooden gate and across a long sloping lawn to the koi pond, expecting to find his unicorn there, maybe drinking, maybe admiring its reflection in the still water, or even lying with legs folded beneath it, tired after a day of exploring.

A trio of little white egrets stood at the rim of the pond, but there was no unicorn to be seen. Billy paused with one foot on the ground and one on the Onewheel, thinking. Was he supposed to call some special call? "Unicorn— Here, Unicorn?" Or maybe whistle a tune? But what would that tune be?

He had seen a flash of white. He knew it. He could go back to search more of the woods, except didn't the unicorn know it was Billy's, so why would it be hiding, if it was hiding?

Or maybe it had been attracted to the clear blue water in the swimming pool.

Or he supposed the story of the maiden might be true and Billy was going to have to find one of those to sit under a tree and trap it. He really hoped that wasn't what was going on.

He rode his Onewheel back to the swimming pool which lay quiet and clear blue in the afternoon sunlight. No unicorn stood on the flagstones that surrounded it, or on the diving boards, or in front of the pool house beyond the shallow end, where flowering jasmine had been trained to grow up trellises and conceal the machinery needed to keep the water clean.

Billy stood at the deep end, trying to have an idea. He was a little surprised not to find his unicorn there, waiting to be found, and a little unsurprised that it wouldn't want to be so close to the house, and a lot disappointed at how difficult this wish was turning out to be. He didn't doubt that somewhere on the grounds a unicorn was waiting for him. He just couldn't think of where to look next. Drawn by the faint flowery smell of jasmine in the air, he rode the Onewheel alongside the pool, and as he rounded the back of the pool house there it was.

He stumbled off the Onewheel.

Billy hadn't guessed how shining and white and perfect a unicorn was. Not a hair was out of place in its long white mane, not the smallest smudge of dirt stained its long white tail. The round eyes—were they green? gold streaked? brown?—and the narrow curves of silver hooves: now that he'd found his unicorn, it was so wonderful he couldn't think of a word to say.

"Billy?" it asked.

How did it speak? It was scientifically impossible for an animal without a voice box to talk, and besides it sounded just like an American. It didn't even have an accent. How could it be a voice that came through the air between them? It definitely wasn't mental telepathy because he heard it in his ears.

"Billy?" it asked again.

Billy could only nod his head, Yes.

"I've been waiting for you. All day," the unicorn said.

"Sorry," Billy whispered. "School," he added, still whispering.

"I know," the unicorn said. "Want a flower?"

Billy shook his head, No thank you.

Could he be asleep, and dreaming? This was too strange to be real, except he wasn't asleep and dreaming, and it *was* real. Gladness burst in him, and he laughed with happiness. "I don't eat flowers."

"I didn't think so."

"But you do? Eat flowers, I mean."

"What else is there?" the unicorn wondered,

reaching its muzzle up to nip another delicate white bloom and chew gently on it.

The amazement of standing beside a real, live unicorn, watching it eat a flower . . . a unicorn! "Where did you come from?" Billy wondered.

"Home," it answered. "You wished," it reminded him.

For a long, silent minute Billy stared at it. His unicorn. The unicorn looked right back at him, out of large round eyes that seemed to shift from green to brown to gold without changing at all.

"What's your name?" Billy asked.

"Name?"

"What do you call yourself? Who are you?"

It thought for a minute, eyes slipping from green to gold to brown, then answered, "I'm I."

"I the letter? Or Eye, the things you see out of?" Billy asked. "Or Aye, like voting for something."

"Yes," the unicorn answered.

"Spelled A-Y—"

"That's who I am. At home." Its eyes filled with silvery tears and it repeated the word, "Home."

"Are you a girl?" Billy wondered.

What would he do with a girl unicorn?

"Yes," she answered the question he asked out loud,

and then the question he had kept to himself. "We can race. Or I could be the king and you could be my knight so we could fight dragons together." Her eyes flashed a fierce golden green.

Did girls fight dragons?

"I'm a boy," the unicorn told him.

"But you said—"

"I am," he maintained.

Billy didn't like things being this confused. "Besides, how could we race. You're way faster than I am."

"You have your Onewheel," the boy/girl unicorn named Ay/Eye/I reminded him. "I could lose."

It didn't understand anything.

"But I do," Ay said. "I understand everything. We all do."

"Are there a lot of you?" Billy wondered.

"Maybe. Yes. Probably. We could race in the woods where nobody would see."

"My Onewheel doesn't work in woods."

"Your feet can run. We like to race. At home. We race no matter where."

"Even where there are lots of trees?"

"I run around trees," Ay explained.

"And bushes?"

"I jump over those."

"Pine and fir trees crowded together?"

"I crash through, or I go around."

"Nothing stops you?" Billy asked, sarcastic.

"Nothing stops me," Ay agreed.

"Really?"

"Really."

Billy laughed again. He kept seeing—over and over, probably he'd never get used to it—how perfect Ay was, perfectly white, perfectly muscular, perfectly friendly, and absolutely magical.

Ay was also perfectly wrong about what a race is. They went deep into the woods, established that the drive was the finish line, used a horn (Ay's) to mark a starting line, and stood side by side behind it. "Ready?" Billy said. "Set?" And then, even though he knew he'd never be able to keep up, "Go!"

They raced side by side.

Side by side?

Billy swerved and sometimes jumped, his feet in their slides landing steadily—thrum thrum thrum— on the uneven ground. He heard the quick twick twick twick of hooves, drumming a much faster beat than his feet could ever match. But every time he looked over to measure the distance between them, the unicorn was level with him.

How could there be a winner in a race like this?

They arrived together at the drive. Billy bent over, hands on his knees, breathing hard. Beside him stood Ay, broad white chest heaving, mane flowing down over the bent neck. If Billy had had the breath for it, he would have laughed again, for the way it felt to run so fast and so hard through such rough terrain, and for how he hadn't lost when he'd thought he was sure to. Mostly, for how perfect his unicorn was. Beautiful, that was the only word for Ay.

Billy straightened up and those brown eyes glinted gold and green at him. "Good race," Ay remarked.

"Perfect," Billy agreed.

THREE

Days passed, each one as wonderful as the one before and many offering surprises of one kind or another. Billy learned that unicorns prefer some flowers to others, and that some unicorns choose by the color and some by the size of the bloom, some only eat one kind of flower but all of them have at least one that they never want to even try. Ay didn't care how sweet the perfume of a rose was, or what color either. "They're what I don't want," the unicorn said, when Billy asked why. "Isn't there something you don't want?"

Billy could think of at least three things like that, especially eggplant.

"And don't you have favorites?" Ay asked. "Jasmine is my most favorite, then after that buttercups are my favorites because they're so little and happy, and dahlias because their colors taste so bright."

One chilly, rainy Saturday, Billy and Ay had to retreat into the pool house, safe enough because in that weather, there was no danger of anyone discovering them there. "Bring a chessboard," Ay told Billy. "And all the pieces."

Billy did have a chessboard and a box holding pieces, but he tried to explain, "I don't know how to play."

"You can learn," Ay answered.

Ay told Billy the names of the pieces and showed him how they could move on the board. After that Billy learned how to set the game up and how to name the moves in the special code of chess, which wasn't that complicated, so that Billy could move Ay's pieces, since unicorns don't have fingers. That much was pretty easy. Hard was figuring out how to play. Game after game, day after day, Billy's king ended up face down on the board. He tried, tried really hard, thinking as hard as he could, but every game ended the same: "Check" then "Checkmate" and Billy's king would be lying flat on his face.

Even when they were doing something they'd done many times before, something could surprise Billy. They ran races in the woods, which Billy neither won nor lost but at the end they were both always breathing heavily. *Can I not lose a race against Ay or can a unicorn not win races?* he wondered, a surprising new way of thinking about what winning and losing meant. Surprising also was how curious Ay was to hear everything Billy knew about unicorns, some of which Ay said was true and some made-up.

"But you came from magic," Billy reminded his unicorn.

"What is magic?" Ay asked.

"Magic is what's maybe not real. It doesn't follow the laws."

"What laws?"

"Of nature. Of science. Magic is what's not possible?" he finally guessed.

The unicorn thought about that, munching on buttercups, which left a dusting of yellow on the shining white muzzle. "So I'm impossible," Ay eventually said. "Except I'm here, aren't I? And there are laws I follow, just not all the same as yours."

"Then what *is* magic, really?" Billy wondered.

Sometimes, they simply wandered, exploring the woods and fields, the ponds and streams, and as they wandered they sometimes told one another old stories. Sometimes one of Billy's old, well-known stories simply confused Ay. Billy learned to notice when that was happening, by the way Ay stared right at him, without blinking, brown eyes worried, trying to understand why anyone would want to put poison into an apple, or why a king would want to be able to turn his own child into gold. "It's a stupid story," Billy would say then.

"Maybe," Ay agreed. "Maybe not."

"Whatever," Billy said. "I'm finished telling it."

"How about a game of chess," Ay suggested.

After a lot of games, the losing began to get to Billy. He tried as hard as he could, planned his moves carefully, thinking and rethinking, but he always ended up with his king face down on the board. One day he'd had enough. "You could let me win you know, even just once," he complained.

"You're a lot better now than you used to be," Ay pointed out.

"I know that," Billy argued. "But all that means is that it takes you longer to win." He was settling the pieces back into their box, white on one side, black on the other, all eight pawns in one row, the king and queen flanked by their court pieces. "Do you always have to win?"

"You don't lose when we race," Ay pointed out.

This was true except, "Because you let me not lose those races," he reminded his unicorn, because that also was true.

When Ay had nothing to say to that, Billy snapped the box closed and stood up, ready to leave.

"Did you ever think," Ay asked, with a friendly golden-brown glance, "that if you take off the L of learn it turns into earn?"

And what did that have to do with anything?

"I have to go," Billy announced.

"No you don't. You want to."

"I'm going," Billy said, and he left.

FOUR

After they'd spent many days together, Billy had a favor to ask. "I want my friends to meet you."

"Why?" Ay wondered.

"Because you are unique. And magical."

Ay had a different idea. "So you can show me off?"

Billy shrugged.

"If anybody knows about me, it's dangerous."

"I'll make them promise."

"I'll have to hide," Ay warned, and the green-brown eyes were worried.

"If they promise, they'll keep you secret," Billy said.

"Maybe. Maybe not. Maybe for a while and then not."

"But you're the only one. That's really special."

Ay wasn't persuaded. "No friends. Nobody else. Only you. I'm sorry, Billy."

"So all I have is not losing races and never even coming close to winning in chess," Billy complained.

"I said I'm sorry," Ay reminded him.

"I know, and I believe you," Billy answered. "But . . ."

"Maybe . . ." Ay started to say, then stopped, and then started again. "Maybe we can do something else together? Maybe you could ride me?"

Billy knew the laws of magic in regard to unicorns. "Unicorns aren't horses. They never have saddles, or reins."

"True," Ay agreed.

"And only maidens ever ride on them and only sideways, and almost never even then," Billy reminded Ay. Maybe his unicorn wasn't aware of the laws of magic, because unicorns lived them.

"Let's try it," Ay insisted. "Maybe a not-maiden can and maybe not, but trying won't hurt. What if it's not one of the laws anymore? Or what if it's not a law for you and me?"

"Can the laws of magic change?"

"Maybe. They're magic, after all. Or sometimes, what people think is a law—of nature or science or anything—actually isn't."

That was true. "Like the way people used to think the earth was flat," Billy remembered.

"Whyever would they think that?" Ay wondered.

But that was the moment when Billy realized what

Ay had offered him and forgot about anything else.
"Yes!" he cried. "Take me for a ride! Where is your
saddle?"

Ay gave a little silver puff of laughter. "You don't
need a saddle to ride a unicorn."

"When can I? Now? Right now?" Billy asked.

"We need to find a big enough rock for you to stand
on, because I'm tall," Ay answered. "And you'll have
to take off your slides. Not right now, Billy. Wait until
we find a rock."

Billy, who had wandered through those woods all
of his life, knew just where to find a big-enough rock.
But when he had slipped out of his slides, climbed up
on the rock, and then pulled himself onto Ay's shining
white back to sit with one leg on each side, he made
the mistake of looking down.

It was a long way down. There was no saddle.

"What if I fall off?" he asked.

"You won't fall off unless I want you to," Ay promised him. "Unless you want to."

"Without reins, how can I steer you?"

"I'll feel it in your legs, or your shoulders might
shift, or you might look in a direction and that will
tell me. And you can let me steer myself sometimes,
when I know better."

"But you always know better, don't you?" Billy asked. "Because you're magic."

"Maybe," Ay said. "Maybe not." He took a small step sideways. Because he was sitting on Ay's back, Billy could feel a tiny difference.

"It's okay, I'm ready," Billy told his unicorn.

"No you're not," Ay argued. "Does it feel perfect to you? It doesn't to me, not yet, you need to shift, only a little, forward—feel the difference? I'll tell you when it's perfect, and you'll tell me. We both have to know."

Billy did as he was told and right away he felt a difference. He felt balanced, and safe. Ay said, "Yes, ready," and they were moving.

In his surprise and amazement and delight and excitement, Billy almost fell off.

Ay huffed softly, laughing. "This is just a trot," he said.

But it wasn't just an anything. It was perfection. Riding his unicorn among the trees of these familiar woods might have been the strangest thing that Billy had ever done in his life—and it was certainly that— but nothing, not one single thing in all of his ten years, had ever felt so right.

It wasn't that riding a unicorn was easy. But he'd never say it was hard. How could anything that felt so comfortable and natural be called hard? The trees flowed beside them, the bushes flowed under Ay's hooves, the shining mane flowed ahead, and beneath him he could feel Ay's strong muscles. Billy was being taken for a ride and he was directing, too; they were together; they moved without any separation between them, the way a breeze dances with leafy branches and which is pulling, which is holding on to, is impossible to know. The way a wave moves on the surface of the water, both its separate self and a part of.

Billy hadn't guessed at this, when he made his wish. How could he have? Now that he had, he thought what a lucky guess his wish had been. His heart felt too big to fit in his chest. This was the best magic ever. This was better than magic.

It was too soon when they trotted back to the mounting stone. (It could never have been too late, not for Billy.) "Tomorrow?" he asked. "Could you go faster? Can I ride when you run?"

"I can't run," Ay answered, sadly. "Not run run. There isn't room here."

"I'm sorry," Billy answered. "I didn't know."

"How can you know when you aren't me?" Ay wondered.

Billy felt a little sad himself—mixed in with all the

happiness. Because he could imagine, now, what it might feel like to his unicorn to use all of those strong, long muscles to really run.

"Let me think," he said. He didn't want Ay to be sad. Not when having his own unicorn had made Billy so happy.

FIVE

Billy thought harder than he ever had before. He fell asleep thinking, and he woke up thinking, and he looked out the car window thinking hard, all the way down the drive to the gates, along busy streets and the long blocks passing the park, all the way up to the entrance to his school: but he couldn't come up with any good ideas. Then, coming home from a day in school, where he had to think about other things, he remembered something Ay had said to him, that first day. "At home, we like to race." Billy remembered that he had wondered about home, at that time; now he wondered about we. And that was his good idea.

It had started to rain that afternoon so he didn't even ask about another ride. They met up in the pool house. "Chess?" the unicorn suggested.

"Listen," Billy said, "when I wished for you? I had two wishes. So I have one left and what if I wish for a friend of yours to come here, too? Or maybe a lot of them? And you can race the way you do at home."

Ay's golden glance was friendly. "They wouldn't like it, Billy," he said. "They wouldn't be right here."

"But you are," Billy argued. "You're right and you like it, don't you? With all the jasmine and buttercups, and dahlias, too, when you feel like them. And the woods."

"I like you," the unicorn answered. "I liked taking you for a ride, even in the woods, and I like playing chess with you. Set out the pieces, okay?"

Billy set out the pieces and played the smartest game he had ever played. It lasted a long time, and he thought of plan after plan, until he figured out that instead of playing to win, Ay was playing to keep Billy from losing.

As soon as Billy thought that, Ay said, "Also you really are a much better player—and you get better every time."

Billy already knew that.

"Are you sure you don't want a friend?" It couldn't hurt to ask again.

"Very. Absolutely. Completely. I promise," Ay answered. "Checkmate."

During the night, the rain stopped. Billy awoke to a clear, bright day. He hoped to get just a glimpse of his unicorn before he left for school—out of his bedroom windows, through the open French doors of the breakfast room, in the woods by the gates—but no shining flash of white was to be seen. On a morning like this, lots of people were out, runners and mothers with strollers, kids walking to school, or Rollerblading or skateboarding or riding their bikes there. Billy's car often had to stop, to allow pedestrians to cross a street. This happened so many times while they were driving along beside the park that Billy reached across and opened the window on the opposite side of the car, so the sweet, fresh air could blow through while he waited.

From where Billy was sitting, even looking through a car window across a line of traffic, you could see long, wide stretches of grass. Next to the entrance was the dog park, where dogs of all shapes and sizes, all colors and ages, too, ran around, tails in the air, chasing, racing, mock fighting or even—in the case of the young, silly ones—circling around themselves, trying to catch their own tails.

They made Billy smile.

They were having such a good time, and two of them, golden retrievers that looked like they could be brothers, ran full speed together, around and around the fenced area, which made him think of Ay, and how it felt to be riding the unicorn, even just at a trot, even just at a careful walk when the undergrowth was thick. Did Ay seriously mean it about not wishing for a friend? Shouldn't Billy do it anyway? Like planning a surprise birthday party for someone.

(Of course Billy knew what he ought to wish for. He wasn't stupid and he wasn't mean. But he didn't want to not have Ay, to talk with, to race against, to ride on, and even to lose to at chess. Billy almost wished he didn't have a second wish because then he wouldn't have to know that he wasn't doing what he ought to.)

Then he had what felt like a whiz-bang, answer-to-everything idea, as the car came to the end of the park and turned right. He no longer saw the houses and stores going by: he saw instead his unicorn, shining white and mane flowing, racing among the trees of the woods with a golden dog running beside it. At the end of their ride that afternoon, he suggested this to Ay. "How would you like a dog? To run with. A golden retriever and he could be your friend, too. That would be fun for you, wouldn't it?"

"I can't have a dog, Billy," Ay told him. "How could I take care of it? Feed it, and dogs need doctors and shots, too."

"I'd help," Billy promised. "I can feed a dog and go with him to the vet. Pick up his messes, too," he realized. That would be sort of nasty, but Ay certainly couldn't do it so Billy would have to.

"Dogs want petting, and scratching, and sometimes training, too."

"I can do all that for you," Billy assured his unicorn.

"Then it would be your dog," the unicorn pointed out.

"Oh. I guess, maybe."

"Probably."

"It's not a good idea then, is it."

Billy's next suggestion came a few days later: "A horse!" Billy cried happily. "I don't know why I didn't think of it before. Aren't horses related to unicorns? Like cousins?"

"They are," Ay agreed.

"Except horses don't have horns," Billy said. "And they're not magic. And they need feeding and cleaning up after, don't they?"

"We're not the same at all," Ay agreed.

More days went by, and Billy kept not wanting to do what he should, and every day he felt a little worse about not doing it. Also, he worried about Ay, if maybe he wasn't as shining bright as before, and maybe wasn't as hungry, even for the delicate white jasmine blooms. Billy almost went ahead anyway and wished for a horse, in case it would make a friend for Ay. But he didn't. He already knew it wouldn't work.

There was one last chance, but it needed bright moonlight. When, in not too long, that happened, Billy told Ay, "I have an idea."

"Will I like it?" Ay asked.

"I hope so. Because when it's night, really late at night and nobody will see us? We can go to the park."

"The park?" Ay asked.

"There's room in the park for you to really run," Billy said. "Open spaces, without trees and bushes in the way. Don't you want to?"

"Can we race there?" Ay asked.

Billy remembered those golden retrievers, racing, and he knew his unicorn was larger and stronger than they were, and also magical. "My idea isn't about racing, because you can't really run—not the way you really can—when you race with me. But I could ride and . . . Let's try it, Ay. You'll see."

"And I can really run there?" Ay asked. "I'll be able to run run?"

SIX

Late that night, had anybody other than the moon been watching, they would have seen something wonderful: a unicorn carrying a boy come out of the woods by the high gates. The boy had neither saddle nor reins and the gates had no power against the unicorn's magic. Unicorn and boy moved silent and smooth as moonlight between rows of sleeping houses. They made so little disturbance that no dog barked, and if a cat hissed, that didn't wake anybody, to look out a window and catch a glimpse of silvery hooves trip-tripping along the empty street. When they reached the park, the creature—it couldn't be a unicorn because unicorns aren't real—turned its head to look back at the rider. It arched its neck and began to canter across the wide grassy space and the long white mane flowed back to brush across the boy's face. Then the creature stretched its neck out long, and really ran.

Only the moon saw this.

Only the boy knew it was happening.

It was only happening to the boy.

As if he were one of the long, smooth muscles, Billy leaned forward. He could feel the joy that flowed from every part of his unicorn's body. He could feel gladness like a wind, blowing all around him as they raced across wide stretches of silvery grass, to swerve around the tall fountain and race back. He could imagine what two unicorns would look like, racing together, how perfect they would be. He could know how right his unicorn felt, running free.

When he knew that, he had to know how wrong everything was for his unicorn, even here in the park, really running. So when Billy returned to his room just before dawn, as the night's darkness was fading into daylight, he opened his sock drawer and took out the little gray rectangle of tissue paper. "I wish my unicorn would go back home," he whispered.

The tissue melted into air and right away Billy wished he hadn't wished that. He even hoped that he'd waited too long to use it so that the magic would be past its sell-by date and wouldn't work. And of course he was sorry not to find his unicorn the next day, feeding on jasmine or buttercups, but of course he was satisfied, and glad, too, that he'd done the right thing.

Even if nobody knew and nobody would ever know. Even if nobody would believe him if he tried to tell them. Even if his unicorn was gone forever.

SEVEN

Billy could have had a horse, but he knew better. He might have nothing to show for his two magic wishes, but he wasn't stupid. He had a riding lesson instead, at the local stables. His instructor was a young woman named Mary.

The instructor stood beside Billy and a groom stood beside the horse—a Morgan, they told him—holding the lead line. It was Billy who had put the bridle over the rust-colored muzzle and fitted the bit into the back of the mouth, who had arranged the reins, one on each side of the head—watched by a dark brown, worried eye as he did so. He'd thrown the saddle onto its back then reached under its belly to buckle the cinch tight.

"Let me give you a leg up," Miss Mary said, "and then I'll check the cinch and adjust the stirrups. You can get used to the feel of being up there while I'm taking care of that."

Billy placed one booted foot into the instructor's

cupped palms and she lifted up. "Throw your right leg over—that's right," she said. While the groom held the lead line, to keep the horse from moving off, she reached under the horse's belly to pull on the cinch, then lifted the right stirrup so that Billy's booted foot slid comfortably into it. Billy sat, and noticed that it didn't feel perfect. Miss Mary came around to adjust the left stirrup. Billy shifted his seat back, just a little. That was better but not yet really right, so he shifted again, moving slightly to the left.

Underneath him, the horse stamped gently.

Miss Mary fitted Billy's left foot into the stirrup and the groom handed her the lead line. "Okay, Billy, just relax and let me walk you around the ring a couple of times, to start with. Are you ready?" she asked.

"No," Billy answered, without thinking. It didn't feel right to the horse yet, he could tell. He reached forward to stroke its strong neck until—after a small movement of the muscles over its shoulders—he knew that both he and the horse were comfortable.

He looked down at Miss Mary. "Ready," he said.

Just for a couple of seconds, she stared at him. She adjusted the reins in Billy's hands. Then "Looks like you won't need this," she said, and unclipped the lead line. "But I thought you said you never rode before."

"I said I never had a lesson," Billy told her, and she nodded.

"Grip with your knees and thighs, if you squeeze gently he'll get started—and if you want him to turn left—"

Billy eased his left leg, gently pulled the reins with his left hand, and the horse walked to the left. He could feel it being patient and he reached his hand down to offer a thank-you pat.

"Keep turning," Miss Mary said, and they did until she said, "Now right, do you want to try a trot? Can you post?"

"Post?" Billy had no idea.

She demonstrated, rising up and down, her knees pulled close, her booted feet apart on the ground. Billy squeezed his knees and the horse broke into a trot and in not many strides he had caught the rhythm of it. When they had made a full circle of the ring and arrived back beside her, the instructor looked thoughtful. "You've already got him working with you, and that's a first in my experience. I'm thinking you might be a natural but—I warn you—however talented you are, you'll have to work really hard. There's a lot to learn."

"Did you ever think," Billy asked, remembering, "that if you drop the L from learn it turns into earn?"

Such things cannot happen.
Everybody knows that.
But what if . . . ?